Danger at Deception Pass

LEWIS and CLARK
SQUAD
BOOK FIVE

Danger at Deception Pass

S T E P H E N   B L Y

CROSSWAY BOOKS • WHEATON, ILLINOIS
A DIVISION OF GOOD NEWS PUBLISHERS

Danger at Deception Pass

Copyright © 1998 by Stephen Bly

Published by Crossway Books
        a division of Good News Publishers
        1300 Crescent Street
        Wheaton, Illinois 60187

Cover illustration: Sergio Giovine

Cover design: Cindy Kiple

First printing, 1998

Printed in the United States of America

Library of Congress Cataloging-in-Publication Data
Bly, Stephen, 1944-
    Danger at deception pass / Stephen Bly.
       p.   cm.—(The Lewis & Clark Squad adventure series ; bk. 5)
    Summary: Tired of practicing basketball every day, the Squad members force Cody to face his terror of an abandoned railroad tunnel, and with the Lord's help he makes it through.
    ISBN 0-89107-985-8
    [1. Fear—Fiction. 2. Christian life—Fiction. 3. Basketball—Fiction.] I. Title. II. Series: Bly, Stephen A., 1944-   Lewis & Clark Squad adventure series ; bk. 5.
PZ7.B6275Dan 1998
[Fic]—dc21   97-32231

06		05		04		03		02		01		00		99		98
15	14	13	12	11	10	9	8	7	6	5	4	3	2	1		

For my good pal
Candice Riggers

One

*T*he air inside the train tunnel felt heavy and damp, like a light fog at night. The toe of Cody's boot caught on a railroad tie, and he stumbled farther into the darkness. After he regained his balance, he jammed his cowboy hat down tighter on his head and kept walking. He could feel a coiled, stiff nylon rope in his right hand.

But he couldn't see it.

I thought this tunnel was only a hundred feet long. How can it be so dark in here? Why can't I see the opening at the east end? Did they close it off?

He stopped and turned his head back. The front opening of the tunnel was no more than a pinpoint of light in the distance.

This tunnel is huge! I would go back if it weren't for the wolves. Wolves? There aren't supposed to be any wolves left in north-central Idaho. But then the tunnel at Deception Pass isn't supposed to be this long either. Maybe this is a mine shaft and not a railroad tunnel. But it was a tunnel when I walked into it.

Wasn't it?

This is stupid.

What am I doing in here?

The coarse, crushed rock from the track bed crunched beneath his feet. When he stopped, he could hear drops of water splashing to his right as they drained inside the granite tunnel. Although the air was a little cold on his arms, Cody felt sweat on his forehead.

Relax, Cody Wayne Clark. Every tunnel has an end to it.

He started to jog into the darkness, caught his toe on a railroad tie, and tripped. The palm of his right hand jammed into unseen sharp rocks; his left crashed into the cold, slick steel of the rail itself. There was a slight, steady vibration in the rail.

Though he couldn't see anything, Cody stood up and brushed off the knees of his jeans.

What made that rail vibrate? The railroad's abandoned, and they won't start salvage operations until September. No one's up here. It's seven miles back to Halt. This isn't funny. I don't want to be here. Where's Larry? Feather? Townie? Denver? Mom? Dad? I thought I was riding my horse. Where's Rolly?

Added to the dripping water was now a faint, dull hum. Cody stopped to listen.

There's a motor back here. Maybe it's a generator for electricity. Someone is mining! I wonder if someone found gold in this mountain and had to wait for the railroad to abandon this line before they could high-grade the ore? They won't want visitors. Maybe I should just hike back out. I can cross Deception Pass some other way. There can't be any wolves out there. Wild dogs maybe. Or a cougar. I'll ride Rolly right over the top of Old Joseph Butte if I have to—provided the critters didn't chase off my horse.

Or was I riding my bicycle? I couldn't ride my bike up Scout Cliff . . . could I? Why can't I remember? How long have I been in here? I can't even remember what day it is or what time of the day!

Cody turned around to look for the speck of light still filtering into the tunnel from the front opening. There was no longer any trace of the tunnel entrance. It was pitch-dark in every direction. In panic he spun around several times but could see absolutely nothing but blackness.

I have no idea what direction to go! I'll have to crawl along feeling the track! This is not good, Lord!

The hum of an engine no longer sounded distant. Sweat dripped off his forehead. Goose bumps climbed the back of his neck.

My rope? I don't have my rope! I must have dropped it. Oh, man, it's my favorite rope! I'm not going back! That's it. No more tunnels for me. I'm getting out of here. I don't care how many wolves there are!

Cody straddled the rail and walked swiftly. He slid his boots along the slick steel. The soft hum of the engine increased. Suddenly his right boot became tangled in something. He reached down in the darkness to pull his foot free.

My rope! I found my rope. What's it stuck on?

Cody tugged and tugged but couldn't get the coiled rope free. Nor could he seem to release his boot.

I can't believe this! This is not a good day!

The motor's hum now became an unseen roar.

Lord, if You're trying to teach me a lesson, I think I've learned it. Never enter anything when you don't know the way out. I've got it. Trust me, this will never happen again. Now if You'd just shed a little light on this situation.

The bright halogen headlight of the train engine flashed from side to side as it approached. At first sight it was so small it looked as if it could have been an exit to the tunnel or someone waving a flashlight.

The railroad bed vibrated.

A train? That's not the light I had in mind. There aren't any trains on this line! They shut it down. It can't be! This is an abandoned line!

When he yanked on his foot, one boot came off. He turned around and began to run the opposite direction of the approaching light. He stumbled, fell, got up, ran, stumbled, and fell again. Now both boots were gone, and he felt splinters from the railroad ties pierce the bottoms of his bare feet.

I've got to make it to the entrance! Oh, man, here it comes! Lord, if You're going to do something, You'd better do it quick!

The approaching train rumbled and roared only fifty or sixty feet behind him. He tried scampering to the side of the tracks. He tripped over the rail and crashed into a granite wall. His hat tumbled into the darkness.

My hat! I'm not getting run over without my hat!

The roaring train engine now looked close enough to touch. Cody dropped to his knees and fumbled for his black beaver felt hat. Instead, his hands touched something soft.

A pillow?

What's my pillow doing in this tunnel?

Now the train was on top of him.

Lord, have mercy on my soul!

Cody dove between the tracks and hugged the pillow to his chest with both arms. Then, for some reason he could not explain, he sat straight up and stared at the rocketing headlight that was only inches from his face.

They won't even find body parts!

Above the terrifying roar of the train engine, he heard a faint voice. "Which one?" it seemed to say.

The light from the train illuminated the tunnel, and he looked to the right to see the shadowy silhouette of someone standing in the doorway.

There's a door! But I don't have time!

The voice was louder this time. "Which girl is it?"

"Girl?"

Denver's voice grew louder than the train. "Which girl were you dreaming about?"

"Girl?" Cody repeated.

His seventeen-year-old brother leaned against the doorjamb of Cody's bedroom. Next to him the dresser was piled high with rodeo trophies and roping ribbons. Dirty clothes were scattered across the brown-carpeted floor. An empty Mountain Dew can perched on top of a stack of basketball cards.

Cody stammered, "What are you d-doing here?"

"Remember me—your brother? I live here. Man, you

are really out to la-la land. I didn't have dreams like that until I was fifteen."

"Dreams like what?"

"Dreams about girls."

Daylight trickled through the beige miniblinds on Cody's window. He stared across the room at the poster of Hall of Fame calf-roper Roy Cooper, who held a pigging string in his mouth as he did a flying off-side dismount.

"Oh, man!" Cody moaned. "It was all a dream!" He wiped the sweat off his forehead and onto his pillowcase.

"From the looks of how tight you're hugging the pillow, I'd say it was a very interesting dream. Who was it you were hugging? Feather?" Denver teased.

Cody tossed the pillow down on the white-sheeted bed. "Feather?"

"Don't tell me you have someone else lined up. I thought *she* was your girl."

"Feather? But she's not . . . I wasn't even . . . oh, man, it was all a dream!"

"You said that before. Now I'll tell you what isn't a dream. Mom's got breakfast on the table, and Dad wants us out there loading hay by 6:30. That means you have twenty minutes, buckaroo."

"Haying? I've never been so glad to load hay bales in my life!"

"Good! I'll see you at breakfast."

"Eh, Denver," Cody called, "how long is that train tunnel on Deception Pass?"

"I have no idea, lil' bro'. No one's ever allowed to go

through there. I guess it might be a quarter of a mile. Why?"

"Oh, it's just . . . I had this dream that it was, you know, a little longer than that."

"You dreamed that you and Feather were back in a dark tunnel?"

"I didn't dream about Feather!" Cody insisted.

"Oh, sure," Denver laughed. "Tell that to your pillow!"

Cody collapsed back spread-eagle on the bed. The sweat on his forehead began to dry.

Dirt and hay dust coated Cody from his boots to his straw cowboy hat. He rode in Denver's Dodge pickup back to the house that evening around 6:00 P.M. He could feel straw bits under his sleeveless black T-shirt, under his jeans, under his socks, under his undies. His eyes stung from dust and dirt, but he didn't have anything clean to wipe them with.

His back ached, his calf muscles throbbed, and his arm muscles burned like they were on fire. Only the top of his forehead above the hat line looked clean as he glanced at the side-view mirror. He ran his fingers through his bushy brown hair, combing out straw and stems.

"We did a day's work today, Cody Wayne." Denver leaned over and rubbed the back of his neck.

"Man, I am tired," Cody admitted.

"Looks like the Squad's practicing at Larry's. You want me to let you out?" Denver slowed down in front of the Lewis home.

"No, I want a shower and to go to bed," Cody groaned. He could see Jeremiah, Larry, and Feather stop playing basketball and wait for him at the end of the concrete driveway. "Oh, let me out here. I'll talk to them for a minute and then come home and get my shower."

"You got it, partner. Mom said to fix ourselves some supper. She and Dad won't be home until after dark. I'm going to take Becky to a movie."

"Really? You mean you aren't totally worn out?"

"Doesn't take much energy to go to a movie. I think I can still put my arm around her and hold hands."

Cody glanced over at his older brother. "Doesn't that distract from the movie?"

"I certainly hope so," Denver laughed as he stopped at the Lewis driveway. "We've seen this film before! And it's certainly better than hugging a pillow!"

"I told you I was not dreaming about hugging Feather!" Cody fumed. He turned to see Jeremiah standing on the running board, his head jammed halfway through the open window.

"You were dreaming about what?" Jeremiah quizzed.

Cody pushed his door open, forcing Jeremiah away. "Nothing! It was a joke. Denver was just teasing me. You heard nothing, Townie!"

Cody's seventeen-year-old brother fogged dust on the gravel road as he rattled past the vacant lot and turned into the Clark driveway.

"What did Denver say?" Feather wore jeans shorts, a T-shirt, and canvas tennies. "Did he say something about me?"

Cody ambled over to Larry and Feather with Jeremiah trailing behind. "He said he was going to the show with Becky tonight."

Larry hiked up his white, baggy University of Indiana shorts, banked in a twelve-foot jump shot, and then retrieved his basketball. "They go to a movie almost every night. There aren't that many new movies to see in Lewiston, are there?"

Feather flipped her long brown hair behind her bony shoulders. "I don't suppose they care what's on the screen!" She stole the ball from Larry and broke for the basket. Her left-handed lay-in came off the rim and bounced back toward Cody. He grabbed the ball.

"Shoot it, cowboy," Larry encouraged.

"Not until he answers me!" Feather jumped in front of Cody and held her hands high in the air. "What did Denver say about me?"

Jeremiah tucked in his brown "Pine Ridge Powwow" T-shirt, which was about the same color as his arms. "He said that Cody had this dream about—" The basketball slammed into Jeremiah's stomach. He staggered back gasping for air. The ball bounced to the dirt. He spun around three times and then tumbled on the Lewises' thick green lawn.

"Whoa! Cody's getting violent! It must have been quite a dream." Larry scooped up the ball and drove for a lay-up.

"Are you all right, Townie?" Cody asked. "I didn't mean to throw it that hard."

"Oh, yeah." He tried to hide his smile but failed. "I

learned my lesson. There's no way on earth I'm going to mention that you had a wild, romantic dream about hugging on Feather."

"He had what?" she shrieked.

Cody pulled his straw cowboy hat clear down over his eyes. *I'm going to die. I'm absolutely going to die. Why didn't that train run over me?*

"Well, Cody Wayne Clark!" she demanded.

He refused to look at her. "Denver was just teasing me. I didn't dream about you," he answered.

Larry chased down the rebound. "Were you dreamin' about some other babe?"

"I was dreamin' about being run over by a train!" Cody fumed.

"Whatever." Larry shrugged. "How about some two-on-two? Or we could go over our game plan for tomorrow night."

"I'm too tired to play," Cody admitted. "We've been haying all day. I'm going home to get a shower and some supper."

"Don't go away mad," Larry called out.

"I'm not mad. I'm just tired."

"Cody, wait up!" Feather called out. She trotted toward him. "I'll walk you home."

"Why?" he asked.

"Because I want to talk to you in private."

They took a few steps across the vacant lot toward the Clark house. "Feather, I really didn't dream about you. Denver made that up. You weren't actually in the dream."

"Oh, it's okay. I know what it's like. Just the other

night I dreamed about Bruce Baxter again." She grabbed her dual-pierced earlobes with both hands and wiggled them as if they were hurting.

"I really did dream about a train running over me."

"I can guarantee you that when I dream of Bruce, it's not about us getting run over by a train." She strutted ahead of him and then turned around and walked backwards. Her giggle died as her voice lowered. "Cody, can I stay at your house for a while tonight?"

He peered into her narrow green eyes. "I guess so. . . . Why?"

Feather's thin face locked tight. "Because my dad's over at the house visiting my mother."

Cody could feel some swallowed hay dust stick in his throat. He almost coughed his answer. "Don't you want to go see him?"

"No." There was absolutely no trace of emotion in her voice. "He brought his girlfriend with him."

Cody tried to look her in the eyes, but she avoided his gaze. "You met her?" he pried.

"Not really. She was still in the car."

"What did your mom say?" Cody rubbed his sore arm muscles. Then he felt self-conscious and dropped his hands.

"Nothing. Mom's working at the store."

"So you just said, 'Hi, Dad. Mom's not here. Bye, Dad'?"

"More or less. He wanted to know when Mom gets off. I told him six o'clock. He said he'd wait. I said I had to come to basketball practice. He said, 'Do you want to meet Brittany?'"

"Her name's Brittany?"

"I guess. Anyway, I said no and took off."

"He's just going to wait at your house?"

"I don't think so. I locked the door. He said he wanted to go out to the tepee and pick up some of his things. What am I going to do, Cody?"

Lord, I can't even imagine what Feather's going through. "I don't have any idea."

"What do you think God would want me to do?"

"Eh . . . I guess He would say, 'Honor your mother and your father.'"

"Which one?"

"Both."

"But how can I? If I visit with Dad, then it's like I'm disloyal to Mom. And if I refuse to go around Dad, it's like I'm dishonoring him. What am I going to do?"

"Eh, maybe . . . maybe you ought to talk to my mom," Cody stammered.

"Yeah, she'll know what to do. Did I ever tell you I'd like to grow up to be like your mom?" Feather reached the front concrete steps of the Clark home before Cody. She spun around and looked down at him.

"I think you mentioned it." Cody sat down on the bottom step and tugged off his work boots.

"Except maybe live in someplace a little bigger . . . and have a job where I could travel . . . and probably wear more makeup than she does and marry someone rich enough to hire a cook and housekeeper . . . and star in a movie and vacation on the Riviera and be independently wealthy—other than that, I want to be just like your mom."

That doesn't sound like my mom at all. "Well, Mom won't be home until almost dark."

"I guess I'll go back and practice with the guys."

"I'm going to get a shower."

"Are you coming back over to Larry's?"

"I'm kind of tired, but I could watch you guys practice." Cody put his hand on the brass knob of the front door.

"Cody . . . "

He turned around.

Her whole face pleaded with him. "Don't tell the guys about my dad's girlfriend, okay?"

"I won't."

"Hey, Cody?"

"Yeah?"

"You know, I mean, I know you weren't, but if you ever did, it would be all right with me."

"Did what?"

"You know . . . "

"No, I don't know," he insisted. "What are you talking about?"

"What you were saying awhile ago."

"About what?"

"You know perfectly well!" she stormed.

"What is the subject here? What are we talking about?"

"We were discussing your dreams about me, you jerk! I just wanted you to know that if, by chance, in the future, you just happened to dream about me, it's okay—even if you dream about hugging me. I won't be mad—that's all!" she shouted and then ran back across the vacant lot.

Twenty-five feet above the pine-needle floor was a three-inch steel pipe parallel to the ground, bolted at each end to a Ponderosa pine tree. Two pulleys were mounted on the middle of the pipe. Each sported a one-inch-thick hemp rope that dropped straight to the dirt, thirty feet west of Cody's house. The ropes stopped about thirty inches short of the ground and were joined together by a sanded redwood plank about two and a half feet long and eight inches wide. Sitting on the plank, wearing a bright pink tie-dyed shirt, cut-off jeans, and black canvas tennies was Feather Trailer-Hobbs.

"Push me higher, Cody!" she thundered.

Cody ran completely under the swing and out the other side in front of her. "I can't reach you anymore," he panted. "That's as high as it goes!"

"I wish I could fly," she hollered down to him.

"You only have to be fifteen years old to take lessons at the airport in Lewiston."

"No, cowboy, I wish I could just launch myself up in the air and fly without an airplane!"

"Oh."

"I'd soar way above the ground and watch everything, but I wouldn't have to be a part of anything. Didn't you ever wish you could fly?"

"I guess not." He shrugged. "Kind of a useless wish since nobody can fly."

"You are the most boring boy I ever met in my life, Cody Wayne Clark!"

"Thank you. Thank you very much."

"You're welcome. Catch me!"

"What?"

Feather jumped out at the top of the swing and flew through the air toward a startled Cody. He quickly held out his arms and braced his feet, putting his right foot behind his left.

The impact was similar to catching a sack of barley seed that tumbled from the top of the truck.

Only Feather was warmer, smoother, and softer.

A lot softer.

"You're also stronger than any boy I ever met," Feather stated as Cody set her feet on the ground. "You're blushing like you never caught a girl jumping out of a swing before."

"I've never caught anyone jumping out of a swing before."

"Well, you have a nice blush."

"What do you mean, I have a nice blush?"

"Sort of shy, yet curious . . . I like it."

"Feather . . . "

She hiked around to the front of the house. "Cody, do you think your mom would let me spend the night at your house?"

Cody trailed along behind. "Probably. You know that she likes having you around."

"Yes, I'm the daughter she never had." Feather's chin

dropped to her chest. "I'm the daughter my father never had, too."

"Hey, you've had good times with your dad. How about that summer when you lived on a houseboat in Puget Sound and protested gill-net fishing?"

"Yeah . . . well, sure, I've had good times. That's the point. When Dad's around, everything is wonderful. But he's not around much. The latest cause always consumes him. Me and Mom are just afterthoughts. And now that he has a girlfriend, he doesn't think about us much at all."

Cody plopped down on the front step. "He came down to see you today."

"No, he came down to get some of his belongings and settle some things with Mom. It hurts so much. Cody, what am I going to do now?"

Cody fidgeted with pulling the hem on his jeans lower on his dusty brown cowboy boots. "Feather, I don't know."

"You're one of the smartest boys I ever met."

"No one ever accused me of being smart. Prescott's smart. Reno's smart. Denver's smart. Me, I'm the baby of the bunch. Just average."

"I don't mean in grades at school. I told you before they don't mean a thing. You have more wisdom about what's right and wrong than any kid I've known. That's what's important, don't you see? It's not what you know, but how you live your life that matters, and I like the way you live your life."

"You do?"

"Yes. Now what am I going to do?"

Cody pulled out his buckhorn pocket knife and began

to scrape dried mud off the welt of his boots. "Feather, one time last year Denver was having trouble with homework, and I teased him and asked if I could help. So he showed me this complicated Algebra II problem. I couldn't even understand the problem, let alone know how to answer it. It was out of my league. Well, that's sort of how I feel now. I feel really dumb. I don't know how to help you. You've got to talk to my mom. She knows a lot about these kinds of things."

"You're right! Mom's still at work. I could go down and talk to her right now and tell her how weird I feel around Dad and how I don't ever want to meet his girlfriend and how I wish the two of them would get things straightened out so I don't have to go through this again. Yeah! I'll just flat out talk to Mom."

Cody felt the tension in his back and neck begin to relax. "That's not exactly what I said, but it does sound like a good idea."

"See, I knew you'd know what to do!"

"But that was your idea. What I said was that you ought to wait and talk to my—"

"Will you go with me?"

"Go with you where?"

"Down to the store to see my mom."

"But . . ." His neck immediately tightened up. "This is kind of private, right? It's the kind of thing for just you and your mom to talk about."

"What if my dad's down at the store?"

"Oh, man. I don't know, Feather." Cody popped his knuckles one at a time.

"Please, Cody. Please come with me!" she begged.

"Well, I'll, eh . . . I'll go to the store, but you have to talk to your mom on your own."

"Thanks, Cody. You know, of course, you're the best friend I ever had in my whole life."

Cody leaned back on the concrete step and stared at the ceiling of the front porch. "I like having you as a friend, Feather."

"Oh, I know that!" She giggled. "Now let's go to the store."

"Right now?"

"Yes. Go get your hat."

"My hat?"

"Your black cowboy hat. Go get it."

"Eh, yeah . . . sure." Cody stood up slowly. His legs still ached from haying all day. "Why do you want me to wear my hat?"

"Because I wrote to Dad and told him my boyfriend was a cowboy."

"Boyfriend!" Cody choked.

"Well, you could pretend for just one night, couldn't you?"

Oh, man. Lord, sometimes real life is even scarier than dreams!

Two

✹

Cody lay flat on his back on the carpet and stared at the living room ceiling. He heard a knock at the front door.

"Come in!" he shouted without moving.

Feather burst through the doorway, her long brown hair braided in a single strand down her back. Cody noticed that her double-pierced ears were adorned with tiny green stones.

"What are you doing?" She strolled over to where he lay and glanced up at the ceiling.

"I'm looking at the future of Cody Clark—hay loader and basketball player," he said weakly.

"And what do you see?"

"I see that he can never survive in both careers at the same time."

"Tired, huh?"

"Tired is for amateurs," Cody replied. "Tired is something that happens after you swim Expedition Lake, or bicycle down to the Salmon River and back again, or have a calf cut in front of you, and your horse rolls on top of you, and the saddle horn stabs you in the pit of your stomach. I am in a higher league than tired—on the edge of total, complete, irreversible collapse is a more accurate description."

"It's a good thing you're resting up before our basketball game."

"I don't suppose you three would like to play tonight without me?"

"You'll feel better in a few minutes," she encouraged him. "Larry says we need your strength under the basket. I hear the Wilderness Wolves are a physical team."

"That means, I suppose, they can't run or shoot worth squat."

"Yeah, that's the rumor. Is your mom home?"

"She's in the kitchen."

"Good. Then I can stay." Feather sat down cross-legged on the carpet next to Cody. "Hey, everything went all right with my dad last night."

"Really?"

"Yeah . . . well, it wasn't, you know . . . good. But it wasn't as bad as it could have been. Mom told him not to bring Brittany to the house, so he didn't. He and Mom had a long talk. That was good, I think. They had me stay up in my room."

"What did he do with her?"

"Mom?"

"No, Brittany." Cody was still on his back, but he glanced over to where she sat. "He didn't bring her to your house, so what did he do with her? Did he dump her out on Main Street and say, 'Wait here. I'll be right back'?"

"I don't know what he did. Maybe she just drove his car around for a while. What difference does it make?"

"Nothing, really. I just wondered what it would be like to be dumped out in a strange town because no one wanted you around."

"Are you feeling sorry for that home-wrecker?" Feather asked.

"Nah, not really. I'm just tired. I guess my mind kind of wanders."

"Anyway, they went back up to Dixie. So me and Mom can get back to finding a routine."

"Is your mom doing all right with that?"

"Here's the funny thing—Mom seems perky, happy, in better shape mentally than I've ever seen her. She left all her herbal medicines out at the tepee, and she hasn't had a bad spell since we moved to town. All she wants to do now is go to work. Mr. Addney's letting her put in overtime, what with some folks on vacation." Feather reached out her foot and prodded Cody's leg. "Now are you coming to the basketball game? Larry wants us to go over a new plan." She jumped to her feet. "They're waiting for us."

"My body says 'no way,' but my spirit says 'get up and go.' Give me a hand." He reached up toward her.

"Oh, you think I'm going to fall for that old line?" she chided.

Cody dropped his hand to his side. His forehead wrinkled. "Did I do something wrong?"

"I can't even tease you, Cody Wayne. You are so . . . so . . . backward and shy you don't even know when I'm kidding."

He rolled over to his stomach, then slowly pushed himself to his hands and knees. "What are you talking about?"

"That's my point. I should have moved to Halt when I was eighteen, instead of only thirteen. Maybe you'll turn out all right in a few years."

Cody struggled to his feet and then stretched out his arms. "Eighteen? That's too old for summer basketball."

"Who's talking about basketball?"

"We are."

"Oh, brother. Come on, Cody Wayne. Let's get to the gym before Larry develops an alternative game plan for us to memorize."

There were exactly fourteen people in the gym when Feather and Cody arrived. None sat in the bleachers.

"Where are our adoring fans?" Larry pondered.

"At home in front of the TV watching the Seattle Mariners," Jeremiah piped up.

"They're going to miss one of the most innovative games of the summer." Larry threw his arms around Jeremiah and Cody. "Do I have a plan for you! The cowboy will do most of the shooting."

"Me?" Cody protested. "I'm not the shooter on this team."

"That's the point," Larry beamed. "They'll be expecting me to take the shots—that, plus Townie's three-pointers. I know for a fact they haven't practiced any plays to stop Cody."

Cody rubbed the back of his neck. His arm muscles ached. "I'm done in, guys."

Larry pulled away and began to dribble the basketball. "Once the adrenaline kicks in, you'll do just fine!"

"I was hoping you could play this one without me." Cody's head drooped a little as he tried to wipe the exhaustion lines off his forehead with the palm of his hand.

"You're the only one on our team who's strong enough to battle the boards with the Wolves," Larry insisted. He reached into his gear bag and pulled out a foil-wrapped pouch. "Here, eat one of these."

Feather wrinkled her nose. "What is it?"

"My lucky fudge."

"All right!" Jeremiah grabbed a large chunk. "If I eat two, will I be twice as lucky?"

"Dream on. There's just enough for each of us to have one." Larry passed the foil package to Cody. "How about it, cowboy? Are you playing?"

"I think I'd do more harm than good. Give them your best shot first. If you need me, then I can come in later. I'm not kidding. I really am worn out. I feel worthless."

Larry took a deep breath and let it out slowly. "All right . . . then we'll have to try our outside game. Feather, you're the next tallest. You play post. If we keep moving, maybe we'll stay out of their way. Try not to get clobbered."

The Wilderness Wolves had a fairly simple strategy. All three members ran straight into whoever was guarding them, no matter who had the ball. At least one of the three defenders would tumble to the ground. The ball was then thrown to the open man, and a basket usually followed.

Larry called a time-out. The score was 12 to 6.

The Wolves had 12.

"This isn't working, cowboy," he complained. "They're playing too rough!"

"If that kid runs into me one more time, I'll punch his lights out!" Feather announced.

"I'll go in for Feather," Cody offered. "But I tell you, I'm about as mobile as a tree."

"I'd like to run my guy into a tree," Jeremiah announced. "I've spent more time on my backside than on my feet."

"Run them into me," Cody suggested.

"What do you mean?"

"Drive them into me. I'm not moving."

"You'll get clobbered," Feather warned. "These guys lower their shoulders."

"I couldn't hurt worse than I do right now. Let's see what happens. Maybe they can't take it as well as they dish it out. If they have a hard collision a time or two, they might change their tactics."

"Hey, talk about taking one for the team!" Larry cheered. "Are you sure you don't want a piece of lucky fudge?"

"Come on, let's get this over. Then I can go home and collapse," Cody urged.

A wiry, quick, red-headed boy named Kyle charged right at Larry the minute the ball was tossed in. Larry sprinted around Cody, and Kyle crashed into Cody's strong shoulder and crossed arms. The Wilderness Wolf tumbled to the floor while Cody remained motionless. Larry spun around and bounce-passed the ball back to Cody who sank a no-jump lay-in.

"He pushed me down!" Kyle complained while pulling himself to his feet.

"He didn't even move," Feather called out from the sidelines.

On the next possession, Cody's man charged at him from one side, Kyle from the other. This left the third Wolf double-teamed by Jeremiah and Larry.

The Wolves lowered their shoulders and almost tackled Cody. Both bounced off him and stumbled to the hardwood gym floor. Meanwhile, Larry stole the ball, and Jeremiah stepped back behind the three-point line. A bounce pass and a set shot later, the Squad had three more points.

"Great going, Cody!" Feather yelled.

Great going? I'm too tired to move. And I refuse to fall over. It would take too much work to get back up. Think I'll just go to sleep under the bleachers when this is over.

The score was soon tied at 14 each, and Cody hadn't moved more than two feet since he came into the game. The Wolves ran one more play to get Cody out of the way. This time Kyle drove around Larry, past Jeremiah, and lowered his shoulder into Cody's stomach.

The result was the same. A Wilderness Wolf crashed to the floor.

Lord, this isn't basketball. It's football. No, it's like that fake wrestling on TV. Bodies bouncing all over.

"That's the second time you knocked me down, Clark!" Kyle called out.

"You tried to clear him out of the key with your shoulder!" Larry insisted.

"I'll clear him out!"

Cody watched as Kyle threw a clenched fist into his jaw. The collision sounded like a two-by-four slamming into a barn wall. Cody's head flew back a little, but his feet remained steady as he just stood there and glared at Kyle.

"My hand!" Kyle cried out. "You broke my hand! Oh, man!"

"If that's your best shot, Kyle, it's just not worth the energy to hit you back," Cody snarled.

"Are you okay, iron-man?" Jeremiah called out as he trotted over to Cody.

The other Wolves huddled around Kyle just as Larry's dad jogged out onto the court, clipboard in hand.

"Kyle, go home and put ice on your hand."

"The game isn't over," the red-headed boy protested.

"It is for you."

"I'm kicked out?"

"Yes. There will be no punches thrown in this league. You know the rules. One more misstep, and you're out for the summer. Have you got that clear?"

Kyle threw up his hands in protest. "But we'll have to finish with just two guys."

"You should have thought of that before you threw the punch," Coach Lewis lectured.

"How about Clark? Why isn't he kicked out? He provoked it. He threw me to the ground twice. You saw that, didn't you?"

Coach Lewis stepped over to Cody. He spoke quietly. "How's your jaw?"

"Oh, it hurts some. But so does every other bone in my body," Cody replied in hushed tones. "I've been haying all day. I'm so tired I can't stand. How about kicking me out of this game so I can go home and rest? They don't need me."

Coach Lewis glanced over at Larry and Jeremiah, then back at Cody. "Are you kidding me? You didn't do anything."

"I know, but with them shorthanded we'll win easily enough without me—and if Kyle sees me kicked out, he won't come back and do something else dumb."

"Are you serious?"

"Please."

Coach Lewis turned around to the remaining Wolves and Squad. "Cody's kicked out of this game, too."

"We want our last time-out!" Larry hollered.

Cody walked to the sideline with the others and picked up his gear bag.

"What did you say to my dad to get kicked out?" Larry asked.

"I told him I wanted to go home and take a nap, and if I got kicked out, you couldn't make me play, and Kyle wouldn't be so ticked."

"Maybe that punch did do some damage," Jeremiah hooted.

"I've seen fights before." Feather shook her head.

"When you grow up going to pickets and protests every day, there are plenty of fights. But I have never seen anyone take a punch with just a sneer. That was totally awesome."

"I was tired."

"Go home, cowboy," Larry commanded. "Look, guys, in this league we can play them if they only have two. So spread it out, pass quickly, take the open shot. On defense, we'll go one on one with Feather in the paint."

As Cody left the gym, he heard Larry's triumphant shout and knew that the Squad had scored a basket. He didn't turn back around.

It was a dumb place to drop your wallet.

While hiking up the narrow trail, Cody had pulled out his wallet to see if he had enough money for an Oreo milk shake when he got back to town. But he stepped on a rock, twisted his ankle, and the wallet tumbled into a hole. The hole was only a couple of feet deep, but Cody had to lie in the dirt to reach into it.

Man, it's deeper than I thought. I can't believe I dropped my wallet in this hole. I'll have to scoot clear in there. I'll be dirty from head to foot. I'm not going to the Treat & Eat all dirty. This thing is narrower than I thought. How come it's dark in here? Where's my wallet? I can't see my wallet.

I can't see anything!

Oh, no . . . I'm stuck!

I've got to be the stupidest guy in town!

"That's what they're calling you, really!"

The voice came from somewhere outside the hole. It was a girl's voice.

"What do you think of that, Cody Wayne Clark?"

A nudge in the rib cage caused Cody to sit straight up . . . in the middle of the living room floor. Larry, Jeremiah, and Feather were huddled around him.

"Whoa, you really were sound asleep!" Larry carried a basketball under his arm.

"Oh, wow, how long have you been here?" Cody questioned.

"What do you mean, here? Like our eternal existence? Or here on this planet? Or here in Halt? Or perhaps here, as in your living room?" Feather teased.

"I guess I was dr-dreaming."

"From the looks of the sweat, he must have been dreaming about being in the desert," Larry guessed.

"Or maybe he was hugging someone in the desert." Jeremiah flashed a full-toothed grin and raised his eyebrows.

"I just dreamed I was stuck in a hole in the ground."

"That happened to me once," Feather remarked.

"You dreamed about being stuck in a hole in the ground?"

"No. I actually got stuck. We were out in the forest hunting mushrooms, and Mother had one of her talk-to-the-trees spells. I was exploring and found a big hole, so I was pretending to be Alice in Wonderland. Only I got stuck and couldn't get back out."

"What happened?" Larry asked.

"A sasquatch pulled me out."

The basketball dropped out of Larry's hands and crashed into the carpet. "A what?"

"A Bigfoot! At least that's what my mother claims. She said she woke up and saw my feet in the air, and this humongous, hairy subhuman was tugging on me. He had just yanked me free when she started throwing rocks to chase it away."

"Hey, that's a cool story." Jeremiah nodded.

"Thank you. Thank you very much."

Jeremiah laced his thumbs into the underarms of his tank top. "Now what really happened?"

"You don't believe me?"

"Whatever." Jeremiah looked down at Cody. "Hey, iron-man, we brought you a victory Oreo shake."

Cody glanced up at Feather. "Really? I was dreaming about an Oreo shake. Now what did you say when you first came in about what kids are calling me?"

"Oh, he did hear us after all!" Feather giggled. "They're saying you're the toughest kid in town."

"Me?"

"Iron-Jaw Clark."

"Well, my jaw is a little stiff."

"Kyle almost died when you took his punch and just stared him down. We figured you needed a nice cold milk shake." Jeremiah reached over and handed it to Cody. "'Course, it's not as sweet as the one I had last weekend."

"Now Townie's dreaming of DeVonne!" Cody joked.

"Not hardly. I was dreaming of a milk shake."

"Thanks for the shake, guys."

"We knew you'd buy one if you were with us. We kicked in the funds," Larry declared.

"That was sweet of you," Cody gushed.

"Yeah, now you owe us $1.84," Larry reported.

Cody reached for his back pocket. "Hey . . . my wallet's gone! It's in that hole!"

"Hole? No, it's right there on the rug." Jeremiah pointed.

"Maybe he's still asleep," Larry put in. "I'm going to shoot some baskets at my house. Anyone want to come over?"

"I've got to get home and baby-sit my little sisters," Jeremiah announced as he headed out the door.

"I think I'd better get home." Feather slurped the dregs of her shake. "I was supposed to finish the laundry before Mom got off work. Did I tell you we bought an electric washer and dryer? They're used, but it's so cool. I just love doing the wash. It's the first washer and dryer we've ever had."

Then, in a flash, they were all gone.

Cody struggled to the kitchen, drank part of the milk shake, and wandered off to bed.

That's the only explanation he could think of for waking up the next morning fully dressed, on top of his covers, with a chocolate taste in his mouth.

"Hey, what are you doing home so early? Did you get fired?" Larry called out as Cody strolled across the empty lot between their houses.

"We finished up one field by noon, and Dad wants to let the other dry a little before we bale it."

Larry kept shooting baskets as Cody approached the Lewis driveway. "So you have the afternoon off?"

"Yeah."

"How's your jaw?"

"What's it look like to you?"

"Like a bruise about the size of a quarter."

"I've been hurt worse."

"You still worn out from all that haying?"

"Actually, I don't feel too bad. I think my muscles are getting used to it. That and about twelve hours of sleep last night."

Larry swished in a hook shot. "Let's get Townie and Feather and practice basketball."

Cody grabbed the ball and tossed up a hook shot.

Nothing but air.

"We don't have to practice every single day." Cody watched the ball roll toward the trees.

"If we're going to be champs, we do. The Ponderosa Pirates are still in first place."

Cody retrieved the ball and held onto it. "Larry, have you ever lived one day of your life and not thought about basketball?"

Larry knocked the ball out of Cody's hands. "Nope. And I don't intend to start now." He tossed the ball over his head to the basket behind him. "All right! Lewis fires up an impossible shot and wins another game."

"I'll go get my bike," Cody announced.

"'Well, Larry, how's it feel to win another game?' 'You

know, Amad, twenty-six times my team has trusted me to take the winning shot at the end of the game. And I've made it all twenty-six times! It's no big deal, really.'"

Larry was still jabbering at his pretend interview when Cody reached his own driveway. *Lord, it's an obsession with him. Maybe he needs to talk to a doctor about it. Maybe there's some medicine or something that would help him. I really like Larry, but he's in such a rut! Lord, thanks for letting me have more than one best friend.*

Jeremiah Yellowboy was sitting on the concrete steps of his blue and white First Street house when Cody and Larry arrived.

"Oh, yeah, now you show up!" Jeremiah hollered at them.

"Did we miss something?" Cody asked.

"No, that's the problem. You're just in time. Do you two have any idea what's in this tin?" Jeremiah held up a round, red three-pound coffee can.

"Coffee?" Cody asked as he dropped his bike to the dirt and sauntered up the sidewalk.

"Hah! What's in here is guaranteed to make you drool. Guess again."

"A two-volume videotape set of the greatest NBA plays over the past fifty years, with narration by Larry Bird," Larry blabbed.

Jeremiah and Cody turned and stared at Larry.

"Well, eh," he stammered, "that would certainly make me drool."

"If it makes Townie drool, it must be something to eat," Cody surmised.

"Yes, but what could make me drool more than anything else?"

Larry shrugged. "You like everything."

"Cody knows my favorite."

"Large, soft coconut macaroons. Your Aunt Lucy sent you some macaroons." Cody plopped down next to Jeremiah. Larry stood in front of them dribbling the basketball on the ice-damaged sidewalk.

"You're only half right. These are the best macaroons on the face of the earth, but my aunt didn't make them."

"Your cousin Honey made them?" Cody inquired.

"Nope. Guess again."

"How can we guess? You're related to half the people in Idaho," Cody complained.

"This isn't a relative, and she doesn't live in Idaho."

"She? Some girl is mailing you cookies?" Larry prodded.

"DeVonne!" Cody hooted. "She baked you some cookies?"

"What can I say? The girl's crazy about me."

"She's just plain crazy." Larry stopped dribbling and tucked the ball under his arm.

"Now, now—don't dis my cookie."

"The macaroon or DeVonne?" Cody teased.

"Both."

"I don't like macaroons," Larry announced. "They have coconut in them."

"That's what makes them so good."

"But it's so—so gritty. All those little coconut slivers get stuck between your teeth, and you have that taste in your mouth for hours. It's disgusting," Larry declared.

"Good! That eliminates one mouth to feed!" Jeremiah's smile revealed coconut between his upper front teeth. "Now if I could convince the cowboy to hate coconut, I'd have them all to myself."

"Forget it. I love coconut." Cody reached for the coffee can. "Give me one."

Jeremiah passed the tin to him. Cody took a golden brown macaroon and looked it over. Then he held it gently beneath his nose and sniffed the sweet aroma.

"Are you going to inspect it or eat it?" Larry admonished.

"Don't rush him," Jeremiah warned. "A work of art needs to be fully appreciated."

Cody took a large bite and slowly chewed.

"Get real! It's just a cookie," Larry complained.

"No," Cody disagreed in a muffled voice. "It's a masterpiece. You are one lucky guy, Townie. How did DeVonne know you liked macaroons?"

"I told her."

"You mean you told her last week when you bought her that milk shake over at Flathead Lake?"

"No, I wrote it to her in a letter."

"You're writing to a girl?" Cody gasped. "What is this world coming to?"

"Hey, I write to Lanni DeLira," Larry admitted.

"Yeah, but discussing basketball stats isn't the same

as having someone bake you your favorite cookies. You don't see me writing to any girl!" Cody asserted.

"That's because your girlfriend lives here in town, and you see her every day."

"Feather? She's not my girlfriend. She's a friend who happens to be a girl—that's all."

"Like Lanni," Larry added.

"And DeVonne."

"Oh, no way. Baking your favorite cookies—come on, Townie. This girl has a crush on the pride of the Nez Perce Nation," Cody jibed.

"Well, if she's that serious, it would be better for me not to share these cookies. It might insult her."

"Whoa!" Cody grabbed another macaroon before Jeremiah jerked the can out of his hands. "Maybe I was wrong. I'm sure it doesn't mean a thing."

Jeremiah pointed at their bikes. "Where are you guys headed?"

"We thought we'd get you and Feather and find something to do," Cody explained.

"We were thinking of having basketball practice," Larry added.

"Why?" Jeremiah mumbled, another macaroon crammed in his mouth.

"Because . . . because," Larry sputtered, "we want to win the league championship in a couple weeks, and we'll need to constantly improve in order to beat the Pirates."

"I say we go down to Buy Rite, latch onto a Mountain Dew, and sit out on the bench playing Cool Rig," Townie suggested.

"Sounds good to me." Cody turned to Larry. "I could use a drink. I've got all these coconut slivers stuck between my teeth, and I . . ."

"Aaaagh!" Larry gagged. "I don't want to hear any coconut horror stories!"

Cody raced out to the bikes. "Come on," he hollered, "let's go see if Feather's home."

Behind a huge spruce tree on a narrow lot on Fourth Street sat Feather's small white house with its peeling paint. For over seventy-five years the Central Pine Company lumber mill had fueled the Halt economy. Company housing consisted of identical, very small one-bedroom homes lined up on twenty-five-foot-wide lots. In many, like Feather's, the attic under the steep roof had been remodeled to provide a second bedroom.

Cody knew it was one of the more modest homes in Halt. But he also knew that Feather and her mother were delighted to be there instead of in the tepee out in the woods.

At one time there had been a gate on the sagging welded wire fence that stretched across the front of the place. Cody leaned his bike against the fence and led the procession to the uncovered front porch. He knocked on the slightly sagging screen door.

"Feather?"

"Hi, Cody! You aren't working this afternoon?"

"Nah, we got caught up."

"How's your jaw?"

"Bruised. It's all right. I was hurt worse when a calf kicked me this spring."

"I'll be right out," Feather announced. "I'm not allowed to have boys in the house when Mom's not home."

Cody, Larry, and Jeremiah sat down on the front porch. Cody called back in through the screen door. "That's cool. We have the same rule at my house."

"I know. That's what I told Mom. You know what else? She said she wouldn't have any men friends over unless I'm home. She said, 'What do you think your Mr. Nice will say about that?'"

"Mr. Nice is influencing the whole town," Larry teased.

"I'm glad you came over," Feather called. "I have a surprise for Cody, and he can share it with you guys."

Cody tried to look through the screen into the darkened house. "What is it?"

"Just wait, cowboy. I'll bring it out."

The screen door flew open. Feather's hair was all tied up on top of her head. She wore a pink T-shirt and cut-off jeans and was barefoot. "Ta-daa! Cody's favorite—Five-Layer River Bottom Bars."

"Oh?" Jeremiah raised his eyebrows. "A girl made cookies for you? Mr. I'm-Above-All-This has a girl making him cookies!"

"They aren't cookies," Feather corrected. "They're River Bottom Bars. What's so funny?"

"Nothing!" Cody stormed. "Absolutely nothing!"

"Well, I thought you'd be a little more grateful," she pouted.

"Oh, I am. Really. You know they're my favorite."

"Feather, can you answer a question for me about girls?" Jeremiah quizzed.

"Townie!" Cody cautioned.

"I'll try," she said.

"Now when a girl bakes a boy his favorite cookies, does it mean she . . . you know . . . has a crush on him?"

"Of course not!" she replied. "It could mean she just wants to say thank you for some kindness. That's all!"

"The defense rests." Jeremiah beamed.

"What this all about?" she asked.

"Oh, DeVonne just mailed a macaroon thank you to Townie," Larry explained.

"DeVonne? From the Browning Bombers?"

"Yeah, but it doesn't mean anything, does it?" Jeremiah insisted.

"Well, it meant she was thinking of you, that's for sure," Feather insisted.

"And you made Cody his favorite cookies," Jeremiah added.

"Bars."

"Whatever."

"But that's different," Feather explained. "I just wanted to thank Cody for writing to me."

"He wrote to you?" Larry gasped. "But you live right here in town."

"Yeah, but I've never had a post office box before, and I've never gotten any mail, so Cody writes to me every week."

"I seem to recall back in the distant past, say, ten minutes ago, some cowboy said he never wrote to any girl," Jeremiah jibed.

"But—but," Cody stammered, "what I meant was, I never wrote to any girl who lives out of town."

"I don't seem to remember him using that phrase, do you, Larry?"

"Oh, no. I definitely think he failed to qualify that statement."

"Writing to Feather doesn't count!" Cody countered.

"Then maybe I shouldn't have baked these for you," she huffed.

"Wait a minute! Wait a minute. What I meant was—"

"Make this good, cowboy, or you're about to be clobbered by a pan of Five-Layer River Bottom Bars," Jeremiah kidded.

"Okay, you guys are right," Cody confessed. "At the time, I was trying to think of any girls who live out of town, and I couldn't think of any. I have written to a girl. And I have had a girl bake me cookies."

"Bars," Feather hissed.

"Right. Do we get to eat them now?" Cody asked.

Feather's eyes looked down, but her nose was turned up. "You squeaked by that time, Cody Wayne."

"Hey, what's in these?" Larry quizzed.

"Graham crackers, flour, milk chocolate, walnuts, coconut, and caramel," Feather reported.

"Coconut! Aaagh!" Larry groaned. "This isn't fair!"

"Hmmph, yuum phorr ussss," Jeremiah mumbled as he wiped caramel off the corners of his mouth.

"What did he say?" Feather asked.

"That makes more for us," Cody disclosed.

"Hey, Clark! What's this about you being the toughest kid in town?" A yellow Jeep pulled over in front of Feather's. J. J. Melton's head stuck out the window.

Three

❋

*O*ne mild July day when Cody was six years old, Mrs. Dressen taught her Sunday school class outside on the back steps of the Halt Community Church. The lesson was about how all boys and girls who had Jesus in their hearts ought to learn to love everybody. At the time, Cody figured it was a rule he had to follow. Over the next seven years of his life he tried.

Seeing J. J. Melton always reminded Cody that he had a long way to go.

Jacob Jules Melton was one year older and twenty pounds heavier than Cody. His dark eyebrows seemed to be painted in a permanent scowl. J. J.'s social skills had not progressed beyond the twelfth century. He talked loudly. He talked often. His vocabulary included all those words that get bleeped out of television network movies.

Cody didn't know about every person on earth, but he was convinced right at this moment that he did not love J. J. Melton. A River Bottom Bar in his right hand, he got up and started walking toward the Jeep.

"Cody, just ignore them!" Feather called out.

"You don't need any help, do you?" Larry didn't move a muscle.

Jeremiah's words came through a whole River Bottom Bar: "Dnnn uphmft frr whmp."

Devin, though too young for a license, was driving the Jeep. Rocky Hammers, wearing a black T-shirt emblazoned "Bad Bob's Bar," sat in the backseat. "You're not the toughest kid in town, Clark!" J. J. challenged.

"Nope," Cody agreed as he approached the vehicle. "I never said I was. I don't know why some kids said that." A big red Irish setter named Paprika, who belonged to the neighbors, trotted up to Cody's side and sat down on his boot.

"We heard you took Kyle's best shot without a flinch and stared him down," Rocky called out from the backseat.

"I was too tired to care." Cody shoved the rest of the River Bottom Bar into the dog's eager mouth.

"Looks like you've got a tattoo on your chin. Does it hurt?" Devin asked.

"Nah, it's kind of like being kicked by a calf. I've had that happen lots of times." Paprika sauntered back across the street.

J. J. jumped out of the Jeep. "Let's see you stand there and take *my* best punch. I can guarantee it will be harder than a calf kick."

"Come on, J. J." Cody took a step back, dragging his boot heel in the gravel road as he retreated. "There's no point in that."

J. J.'s neck and face flushed. "Then you aren't the toughest kid in town. That's the point."

Cody stopped backing up and locked his knees. "I never said I was."

With both fists clenched, J. J. leaned forward. "Kids are claiming it."

"I tell you what, J. J., if you promise not to believe what they say about me, I won't believe what they say about you."

Rocky let out a loud whistle and hooted, "Hey, that's fair!"

"What did you mean by that?" J. J. fumed.

"He meant, relax, chill off, have a River Bottom Bar."

Cody whipped around. Feather held out the cookie pan to J. J.

"Are you talking to us, broomstick?" J. J. snarled.

"These are really good." She shoved the pan into the open front window of the Jeep. "Help yourself."

Rocky and Devin each scooped up a large bar. Then she brought the pan back and held it for J. J. "You'll like them. Really," she encouraged. "Besides, Cody can't control what some kids say about him any more than I can control what you say about me."

J. J. took one of the chocolate caramel brownie bars. "If I beat the tar out of Clark, that will change what they say about him."

"But what would they say if he beats the tar out of you?" she countered.

Cody tensed. *Feather, don't. . . . Don't tick him off any more!*

"Hey, these are really good!" Rocky licked his fingers.

"Thanks." Feather pushed the pan back inside the window. "Have another." Then she turned back to J. J. "Think about it. What if Cody only had a one-in-ten chance of whipping you in a fight? Things like that happen. It wouldn't be worth the gamble. You're the tough guy around town now. Why blow it? Have a River Bottom Bar. Relax."

"I don't want anything you cooked!" J. J. ranted.

"Hey, can I have yours?" Rocky called out.

J. J. threw the bar to the gravel roadway. "No, you can't have it!"

"That's not cool!" Rocky called out

Paprika loped over and sniffed the dirty brownie.

"I'll tell you what's not cool," J. J. fumed. "It's you two jerks sittin' in the Jeep with crumbs on your faces!" He turned back to Cody. "Tell the kids to stop calling you that, or we'll have a real contest to prove who's tougher."

J. J. crawled back into the rig. Devin raced the engine of his brother's Jeep, and they spun gravel and dirt into the air. Feather stepped back toward the yard. She pulled her T-shirt out from her stomach to protect the brownie bars from the cloud of dust. Cody trailed along behind.

"I can't believe J. J. threw one of those to the ground," Jeremiah called out as they approached the porch.

"I can't believe J. J. didn't slam-dunk you," Larry added.

Cody glanced at Feather. "I can't believe you fed them your River Bottom Bars."

She skipped to the top step and looked down at him.

"I read in my Bible somewhere that you're supposed to feed your enemy. J. J.'s our enemy, so I fed him. At least I tried to feed him."

"J. J.'s not my enemy," Cody insisted. "I don't have any enemies."

"He wants to hurt you. Just what, exactly, do you call that?"

"I just try to ignore J. J. That's all." Cody heard his own words come out flat and unconvincing.

"He doesn't try to ignore you. You might not be his enemy, but he is yours. That's why I gave them the brownie bars," Feather lectured in a school teacher's tone of voice.

"Hey, are we going to play Cool Rig or not?" Larry piped up.

"I've got to clean up the kitchen." Feather's thin shoulders and neck began to relax. "It's kind of a caramel-choco-late-flour mess."

Cody noticed a fat white cloud sailing across the blue July sky. "I don't feel much like it now. I was thinking of hiking around Expedition Lake."

Feather rubbed her freckled nose with the back of her hand and left a white-flour smudge. "By yourself?"

"Cody is never by himself," Jeremiah teased.

"You guys are invited. We've never really gone on a hike together. We ought to do that."

"You know where we ought to hike sometime?" Jeremiah stood up next to Feather. "We ought to hike the tracks from Gray Wolf Crossing over Deception Pass. Cody and I always wanted to—"

"No!" Cody barked.

"I don't mean today." Jeremiah shrugged. "I meant sometime when we have a picnic lunch, canteens, and a fresh supply of River Bottom Bars."

Sitting on the concrete step and dribbling the basketball, Larry remarked, "Isn't it dangerous hiking on the railroad tracks?"

"That's the point. The line's been abandoned, and they'll start salvaging this fall. If we don't hike it pretty soon, it will be gone." Jeremiah glanced down at Cody. "That sucker's over 100 years old. It's part of history."

"Would we walk across those high wooden trestles?" Feather asked. "That looks scary."

"They have pedestrian planks along one side. Me and Cody rode our bikes across them one time. Didn't we, cowboy?"

"No!" Cody blurted out.

"What do you mean, no?" Jeremiah continued. "Remember that time we—"

"I meant, no, we are not going to hike over Deception Pass."

Feather put her hands on her hips. "What's the problem here?"

"There's no problem. I'm not hiking over Deception Pass . . . ever!" Cody headed back toward his bike. "Now who's going with me around the lake?" he snapped.

No one replied.

"Good. I'll just go by myself."

Cody didn't look back at his dazed friends as he rode up Fourth Street.

The old, rusted iron footbridge at the back of Expedition Lake groaned as Cody hiked out to the middle of it and paused. He stared back across the lake at Halt, Idaho, and the reflection of the wooded shoreline in the water. The small, puffy white clouds sailed across the water like headless swans. A slight breeze from the northwest felt cool as it drifted across the water, causing only a slight ripple.

Cody climbed up on the bridge railing and tried to peek down at his own reflection.

I need to comb my hair. "Hey, kid in the black T-shirt! I hear you're the toughest kid in town. You might be the only kid who was called tough for refusing to hit someone back. Well, I happen to know you aren't so tough. You're scared spitless to hike through the tunnel at Deception Pass. You're just playing a game—a game you can't win. One of these days J. J. will whip your tail, and then you'll just be a not-so-tough, not-so-talented, not-so-smart ordinary kid. What do you think of that, Cody Wayne Clark?"

Cody climbed down from the iron railing of the footbridge and tramped east on the narrow fishing trail.

Lord, I'm not having fun. Summer's kind of dragging on. I wish it was time for school. I don't know why none of them wanted to come for a hike. It's the first day I've been lonely all summer. On the other hand, I'm glad they didn't want to hike with me. Sometimes I just like being by myself. I ought to saddle up Rolly and go for a long ride. Maybe Dad would let me take a bedroll and sleep down in the canyon. As long as I stay away from . . .

Lord, I don't understand dreams. I don't know why I

keep getting afraid of tunnels and things. It's like it makes me nervous about everything else.

Maybe I'm just tired.

A nap in the sun on Arrowhead Butte would be nice.

Real nice.

A mile behind the boat ramp at Expedition Lake is a treeless hill named Arrowhead Butte. The north slope of the little mountain is gradual and has enough topsoil to support thick wild grasses. On a summer day when the breeze dries the dew and the bugs are busy somewhere else, the butte offers a nice, private place to think. This was Cody's first hike to Arrowhead Butte for the summer.

With a tall stalk of grass in his teeth, he flopped back on the hillside, propped his hands behind his head, and closed his eyes. The wild grass surrounding Cody was at the green seed stage, and it towered above him.

When a person is tired, sleep is wonderful.

When you are extremely tired and really, really sleepy, falling to sleep is a life-or-death matter.

In less than two minutes, Cody Wayne Clark was sound asleep.

With the blink of an eye, Cody stared straight up at a graying sky. The sun had fled to some hiding place in the west, leaving a red blanket on his face and arms. The dirt felt much harder than when he had lain down.

Lord, that's the first time in a week I've slept without dreaming. It felt good. Really good.

"Then you agree this is where we should turn 'em loose?"

Someone's down the hill! Cody lay flat on his back and listened.

"If they catch us, we'll be arrested."

Arrested for what?

"We'll be in Oregon before they know anything about it. I told you I know a hidden road out here."

They don't see me. Oh, man, I hope they don't see me!

"You think they'll be safe back here?"

Lady, just what exactly will you be bringing back here anyway?

"It's got to be a whole lot better than what they have now," the man's voice explained. "Besides, we have to do something. The election's a week from Saturday."

Election? I thought all elections were on Tuesdays.

"How will they know we did it?"

Who's they? Who are you trying to impress?

"They'll know. I'll call the media. Shall we find a backup location?"

"Nope. This one's ideal. We aren't more than a mile away, and no one even knows we're here."

Actually, one person knows you're here—whoever you are.

"What did you put down on the campground receipt?"

They're staying the night in Expedition Lake Campground?

"Mr. and Mrs. L. Skywalker from Roswell, New Mexico."

Yeah, and you call your car the Millennium Falcon, right?

"But they'll know those are phony names."

She sounds smarter than him.

"We'll be on the road before anyone reads it."

On the road to where? Are you going back to Oregon now?

"Be sure and use a different name next Monday night."

"Monday night we'll be Mr. and Mrs. Clyde Bonnie."

I don't get it.

"Like the gangsters, Bonnie and Clyde?"

I still don't get it.

"Yeah. What do you think?"

"I think we better make sure we don't get caught."

I wonder if they're carrying guns?

"That's the beauty of it. No one knows but you and me."

Lord, I don't think I ought to be hearing this.

"Maybe we ought to hike on up to the top of this hill and look around."

Oh, man . . . that is a horrible idea! Maybe I can outrun them. I hope they don't have a gun!

"Nah, let's get back to camp. Planning always makes me hungry."

Cody listened to the retreating cushioned footsteps.

Then he waited some more.

Finally, he sat up and peered across the hillside. There was no one in sight.

I don't know who it was, what they were plotting, or

what to do now—except to go home without being seen. Which should be a piece of cake.

Cody stayed away from the fishing trail, cut through the cedar thicket, climbed through the barbed-wire fence twice, and hiked on through the back side of the slaughter house ruins and across the lumber mill property.

He saw absolutely no one until he walked into town. Del Kellerman waved at him from the gas pump at the Guzmans' minimart where he was purchasing gasoline for his lawn mower. "I'm rooting for you, Cody!" he called out.

"Thanks, Mr. Kellerman. Our team's in second place so far."

"Oh, I don't mean that. I mean the big fight," the bald-headed man shouted.

"What fight?"

"I heard you and J. J. are going to put on the gloves and have it out down at the gym."

"Who told you that?"

"What's the name of the littlest Germaine kid?"

"Kelly?"

"Yeah. She told me about it. Good luck, son!"

Cody slumped home. He tried to be quiet as he entered the front door of the Clarks' tri-level house.

"Cody Wayne, is that you?"

"Yes, ma'am." He entered the kitchen.

"Where have you been?"

"Around the lake, like I said."

Margaret Clark sat on a wooden stool, a laptop computer on the counter in front of her. "You took a long time."

"I took a nap up on Arrowhead Butte. Listen, I heard—"

"Let me tell you what I heard," she interrupted. "I heard that you are planning to fight J. J. Melton to prove who is the toughest kid in town."

"Where did you hear that?"

"At the post office, but it doesn't matter where I heard it. You are not going to fight any kid anytime—if you can help it. Do you understand?"

"Yes, ma'am. I don't know who's saying those things, but I don't aim to fight him."

"Good. Look at this, Cody." She pointed to the screen of the laptop. "Dad won't like this."

He glanced at the screen. "Cattle prices down again today?"

"They dropped six cents a pound in Kansas City." She left the computer on while she sliced homemade bread. "Denver and Dad are trying to fix that old baling machine. I'm taking some supper out to them. You want to go with me? Or would you rather eat here?"

"I'd just as soon stay home if it's all right."

"Yes, and you can talk to the boys when they call."

"Prescott and Reno are calling tonight?"

"They should have some results from the rodeos in Window Rock and Flagstaff."

"When are they coming home?"

"They talked about coming up after the Caldwell Night Rodeo, but I have my doubts." She stepped over closer to Cody. "You got your forehead sunburned, young man."

"Yeah. I should have worn my hat."

"Grab me a six-pack of Cokes from the downstairs fridge while I comb my hair."

"Okay, eh . . . Mom, do you and Dad have any enemies?"

"Enemies?"

"Yeah, those actively working against your best interests."

"You mean, besides Satan, the IRS, the BLM, and the county assessor."

Cody jammed his hands into his jeans pockets. "I'm serious."

"So am I." She jogged up the stairs toward her bedroom, then turned back. "Honey, from time to time people do spiteful, hurtful things. I suppose for a while they're our enemies. But that's the way life is."

"Yeah, it's just that—"

"I can't hear you, Cody," she called from the bathroom. "We'll talk when I get home."

"Yeah," Cody mumbled. "I need to talk to someone."

Cody had just finished eating a cold turkey sandwich with lettuce, tomato, mustard, kosher dill pickle, and Swiss cheese when the doorbell rang. He could hear a basketball bounce even before he reached for the handle.

"Hey, cowboy—whoa, you look a little sunburned. You want to come over and shoot some buckets?"

"Eh . . . yeah and, eh, no."

"Yeah and no what?"

"I got sunburned, but I can't go shoot baskets. Mom

wants me to wait and answer the phone when Prescott and Reno call."

"How are they doing this week?" Larry asked.

"I think they both won some money in Arizona."

"Well, after they phone, maybe you can come over."

"Yeah." Cody stepped out on the covered concrete porch with Larry. "Hey, you want to hear a really weird thing that happened to me this afternoon? See, I went to sleep on Arrowhead Butte, and—"

"And you had another dream about being stuck in a dark tunnel?"

"No! That's the thing. I didn't dream at all."

"Didn't I tell you you'd outgrow it? I was really scared of the dark when I was young. Then one day I said, 'Hey, this is dumb,' and it hasn't bothered me since."

"But this is different."

"I know." Larry retreated across the yard. "But you'll get over it."

"But there was something else I wanted to tell you about," Cody hollered.

"Tell me later," Larry shouted. "Why don't you call Townie and Feather to come over too?"

"Yeah . . ." Cody's voice trailed off.

Cody tapped his finger on the counter as he punched the number into the cordless phone. A familiar voice answered.

"Hey, Townie, what are you doin'?"

"Hi, cowboy! I hear there'll be a big boxing match after the basketball game Monday night."

"Me and J. J.?"

"Yeah."

"Where's this all coming from? I don't want to box J. J. I don't want to fight anyone."

"I guess J. J.'s talking it all over."

"Well, I'm not going to fight him. This whole thing's stupid."

"I agree with you there. But if anyone was ever going to put him in his place, you might be the one."

"Why me? Why not the pride of the Nez Perce Nation?"

"'Cause I'm a wimp."

"J. J.'s older and bigger than me."

"Yeah, but you're cowboy-tough, right?"

"I've had more accidents and more bones broken. Is that what you mean?"

"Maybe."

"Well, I'm not fighting him."

"That's cool. Is that why you called?"

"You want to go to Larry's house and shoot some hoops?"

"Nah, my grandpa's here, and he wants to go fishing at the lake."

"That reminds me. Let me tell you about something strange that happened to me at Arrowhead Butte this—"

"Hey, tell me in the morning," Jeremiah interrupted. "Grandpa's going out the door right now. See you tomorrow, cowboy. Stay out of fights."

"Yeah . . . I'll see you . . . after work."

Cody wandered up to his bedroom and flipped on the ceiling fan. He jammed the heels of his boots into the wooden bootjack on the brown-carpeted floor and yanked off his boots. He tugged off his socks. With a big sigh, he flopped on top of the blue quilted comforter.

He lay on his back and watched the slowly circling oak fan blades. The motor made a slight, constant hum, almost a buzz. He shoved his hands straight out to the edge of the bed and felt the fan breeze wiggle the light brown hairs on his arms.

Man, I wish Feather had a phone. She'd listen to me. Lord, right when I need someone to talk to most of all, there's no one around.

Besides You.

This would have been a good week to skip. I should have gone to Rodeo Bible Camp or something. I heard things I didn't want to hear, somehow got involved in a fight I don't want, and suddenly have nightmares about something that has never scared me before.

Lord, if life is a great big room . . . well, I just want to go over to the wall and watch. Please don't push me out there into the middle.

I'm no good at it.

The ceiling fan continued to whirl in its mad circle. Then Cody heard the doorbell ring. He jogged down the stairs and swung open the door.

"Hi, Cody!"

"Feather! Boy, am I glad to see you!"

"Whoa, the shy cowboy is enthusiastic! This is a surprising turn."

"What?"

"Don't you know it makes a girl feel good when a boy is eager to see her?"

"Oh, yeah?"

"Yeah. You forgot to bring home the rest of your River Bottom Bars." She shoved a foil-wrapped package into his hand.

"They are all for me?"

"Except for the ones already eaten or thrown on the ground."

"My folks aren't here, so I can't invite you in. But I really need to talk to you. Can you please stay for a while?"

"I don't believe this!"

"What? Did I do something wrong?"

"The first time all summer you're happy to see me, and you want to talk—and I have to go."

Cody's heart sank. "What do you mean, you have to go?"

"Mom's out in the car, and we're going to Lewiston to shop."

"Shop? This late?"

"With Mom's long hours, it's the only time she has."

"I really *do* need to talk to you," Cody heard himself urging.

Feather glanced out at the waiting car. "I've hardly gone shopping ten times in my whole life!" She stared Cody straight in the eyes. "But I'll stay if you want me to."

Cody leaned back on his heels. "Eh, nah . . . no, it's okay. Maybe we can talk tomorrow."

"Sure! What time do you want me to come over?"

"Oh, well, I think I have to work tomorrow, so it will

be sometime in the early evening. But it won't matter . . ." His voice trailed off to a whisper.

"Thanks, Cody. And thanks for being so happy to see me. Most of my life people have only been happy when I left." Feather scampered to the car. Cody waved to Mrs. Trailer-Hobbs and watched the green rig back out of the driveway.

He sprinted for the ringing telephone, leaving the front door open.

"Hey, Meathead, how's my main man?"

"Hi, Reno. Mom said you were going to call. How did you and Prescott do in Arizona this week?"

"I tied one in 8.1 in Flagstaff."

"That's cool. Did you win first?"

"Nope. I broke the barrier. But we both won money this week. Can I talk to Mom or Dad?"

"They aren't home. Dad and Denver are trying to fix the baler, and Mom took them some supper."

"I've really got to talk to them. Jot down this number, and have them call me when they get home."

Cody grabbed a black marking pen and wrote the number on the phone book. "Is this a motel?"

"Nope, it's the hospital."

"Hospital!" Cody choked. "What happened?"

"Big brother decided to roll his horse tonight. Probably only cracked ribs or something, but they want to keep him overnight. Have Mom call me, okay?"

"Right. Eh, Reno . . . can I talk to you for a minute?"

"Hey, I've got to get back and be there when the X-rays

come back. You're not having trouble with that cute new girlfriend? What's her name . . . Heather?"

"Feather. How did you know about her anyway?"

"Denver's told us all about it."

"She's not my girlfriend."

"She is cute, right?"

"Yeah . . . in a girl sort of way."

"And she likes you, right?"

"Well, yeah, sort of, I guess."

"Little Bro', you got yourself a girlfriend. Treat her good, you hear? If you don't, you've got three brothers that will take you out behind the barn. I have to go. Have Mom or Dad call me, all right? I'll be at the hospital waiting room all night. It's cheaper than renting a motel room."

Cody stared at the black phone humming its dial tone. Then he hung up. He turned back toward the front door and spotted a large, tailless gray cat sitting on the carpet at the foot of the stairs.

"Hey!" Cody hollered. "Get out of here! Go on!"

He ran at the cat. But instead of sprinting out the open front door, the shaggy animal bounded up the stairs.

"You can't go up there!" he bellowed. "Come on, cat, get out of the house!"

The frightened animal darted into Cody's room and dove under the bed.

"No!" Cody shouted as he flopped on the floor and stuck his hand into the darkness of dust, lint, socks, and cat. Immediately, he jerked his hand back.

Three deep, bloody scratches trailed across the back of his hand.

This isn't happening to me.
This day isn't happening to me.
This week isn't happening to me.
This life isn't happening to me!

Four

The sun blazed down from straight above in an absolutely clear blue north-central Idaho sky. The Squad was gathered around Cody on the concrete steps of the Clark front porch.

His black felt cowboy hat was perched on the back of his head, his dirty nylon rope coiled in his hand. His sleeveless black T-shirt showed a calf-roper and the caption: "The Greatest Show on Dirt!"

Jeremiah's bright white teeth flashed in his smile. "They're going to turn what loose?"

Cody shrugged. "I don't have any idea. But that's what I overheard."

Feather wore a long-sleeved Western shirt tied at the waist over her light blue T-shirt. Her hair hung in a ponytail down her back. "Let me get this straight." She bit on a fingernail. "Some people—you don't know who—are going to turn something loose—you don't know what—and it will change the outcome of some kind of election?"

"And the whole thing is a felony?" Larry dribbled up the steps and back down again.

"Yeah. Is that weird or what?"

Jeremiah jumped straight off the step into the grass. "Alligators!" he shouted.

Feather brushed a metallic-green bug off her knee and leaned against a post on the porch. "Alligators?"

"They're going to turn alligators loose in the swamps behind the lake. Cody, didn't I always tell you those looked like alligator ponds? I saw this movie once where small alligators were accidentally dumped in this abandoned city swimming pool, and they grew bigger and bigger until people started missing their dogs."

"Oh, yuck," Feather groaned.

"Then one day this six-year-old boy didn't come home, and all they found was a—"

Feather put her hands over her ears and shouted, "I don't want to hear this!"

Cody stepped onto the grass with his old brown lace-up Roper boots and began to build a loop with his rope. "Well, it's not alligators. We're at 4,000 feet elevation in the forest. They'd freeze up here."

"I don't think turning an animal loose is a felony, is it?" Feather questioned.

Cody lassoed the sprinkler in the middle of the lawn and then went to untie his rope. "That's what I can't figure."

"I knew a kid once named Floppy who loved animals, and one time—," Feather began.

"Floppy? What kind of name is Floppy?" Jeremiah

croaked. "What a rip! Some guy has to go through life with the name Floppy."

"Girl. My friend is a girl."

"Oh, well, that's okay then." Jeremiah chuckled. "It's definitely a girl's name."

"That's a sexist remark," Feather snapped.

Jeremiah raised his eyebrows. "It is?"

"Yes. Why do you insist that there are boys' names and girls' names? Why can't there just be names, period?"

Jeremiah scratched his head and then tugged on the shoulder straps of his Chicago Bulls tank top. "I don't know. It's just that in the back of the big dictionary at school there's a section that lists boys' names and another for girls' names. I always figured there were officially only two categories."

"And you wonder why I'm home-schooled," Feather retorted. "If a dictionary is that biased, can you imagine what the textbooks would be like?"

"Maybe Feather's right," Jeremiah said. "Why shouldn't girls all over America be named Larry Bird?"

"Ahhh!" Larry screamed. "You're kidding me! That's—that's . . ."

"That's what?" Feather huffed.

"That's totally unfair!" Larry groaned.

"You guys have just been brainwashed."

Cody built another loop with the rope. "Well, it might be okay, but it would take some getting used to—having a guy named Jessica or Rebekah or Elizabeth."

"How about a girl named Arnold, Frank, or Roscoe?" Jeremiah added.

Larry tossed his basketball from one hand to the other. "Anyone named Roscoe would be weird."

"See? There are just names, that's all," Feather asserted. "Some sound good to us, and some don't. But all of that is based on what you're used to."

"How did we get on this subject?" Cody quizzed.

"I was going to tell you about my friend Floppy."

"Did Floppy have a last name?" Larry plopped down and began retying his Nikes. Suddenly he straightened up. "Disc!" he shouted. "Her last name was Disc!"

"Floppy Disc!" Jeremiah hooted. All three boys howled.

"That's it. I'm going home!" Feather stormed off the porch and across the yard.

The loop seemed to drift in the air above her and then float down around her waist like a woven belt. Cody tugged the rope gently back toward the house. "Wait!" he called. "I really want to hear what Floppy did."

"I can't believe you roped me!" Feather fumed.

"I can't either," Jeremiah teased. "That means you two are going out. When a cowboy ropes a girl, it's extremely serious."

"It is?" she asked, holding the rope at her waist so it wouldn't drop.

"No!" Cody blurted out. "It doesn't mean that!"

"I'm yours, cowboy! Shall we set a wedding date?"

Cody felt his slightly sunburned face get even redder.

"I think he stopped breathing!" Jeremiah hollered.

"Relax, Cody Wayne." Feather giggled.

"I just want to know about Floppy, please. What did she do?"

Feather let the rope drop to the grass and strolled back to the steps. "She turned the bunnies loose."

Cody recoiled his rope. "Bunnies?"

"A lady named Nemmingham was raising rabbits in her backyard, and Floppy considered herself a radical animal rights person. So she snuck into the yard one night and set the bunnies free," Feather explained.

"Set my bunnies free!" Jeremiah chuckled. "Just like Moses!"

"What happened to her? Did she get caught?" Larry asked.

"Nope. No one knew who did it, except me."

"What happened to the bunnies?" Cody asked.

"That's the bad thing. One got run over by a beer truck. One drowned in a neighbor's swimming pool. The dog killed a couple, and they never found the other one."

"Freedom isn't all that great!" Jeremiah asserted.

"Well, there aren't any bunnies in town that I know of. And certainly there aren't any over behind the lake," Cody put in.

"The wolves! It's got to be the wolves," Jeremiah blurted out.

"First alligators, now wolves!" Larry scoffed.

"No, really! We've got wolves right up the road from the lake," Jeremiah contended.

"You think someone's going down to the Wolf Education Compound and let the wolves out?" Cody asked.

"Yeah!"

"But that's several miles away from Expedition Lake. How are they going to transport them to the lake?"

"Very carefully," Jeremiah joshed. "I don't know. Maybe they could coax them into the back of a van or something."

"So we'll have wolves in the woods. We already have bears, cougars, bobcats, and coyotes," Larry declared. "This whole topic is a waste of time. Let's go practice basketball."

"But we have to do something about this!" Cody insisted.

"Why? We don't know if, when, how, or where. Come on, guys, I was watching a rerun of the 1983 NBA Championship and saw a play that will work for us. We'll have to adjust the slam-dunking part of it, but other than that—"

"Larry, it's the first of August. We don't need any more new plays," Cody protested.

Larry tucked the ball under his left arm and waved with his other. "You're kidding, right?"

"Not really. I think I'm getting burned-out on basketball." Cody roped the sprinkler again.

"I'll pretend I didn't hear that," Larry replied.

"You heard it. It's getting to be too much like work. What happened to the fun? I could use some fun," Cody declared.

Larry dribbled on the porch. "The fun's in the winning."

"So there's only supposed to be fun in the destination, not in the journey?" Cody queried.

"Now you're starting to sound like one of those boring commercials on TV," Larry scolded.

"That's me. Boring Cody Clark."

"Hey, guys!" Feather interrupted. "Chill off. We're picking on each other too much. We're all on the same team, remember?"

"Maybe we've just been spending too much time together," Cody ventured.

Jeremiah sprang to his feet and brushed off the seat of his black Chicago Bulls shorts. "Are you telling us to leave?"

"I'm just saying everyone ought to have the freedom to do whatever they want and not be pressured by the others to do something they don't want to. We aren't all identical."

"Yeah, well, I think I'll go home and finish building my rocket," Jeremiah announced.

"I've already wasted an hour of practice time," Larry put in. "Basketball may not be very important to any of you, but it is with me."

"This is depressing. I'm going to go read something cheerful—like a Russian novel!" Feather turned to go.

Without another word, all three fanned out across the Clark front yard.

Cody stared after them. *Lord, what's going on here? I can't let this happen!*

"Hey, guys . . . wait a minute!"

Feather turned around and shielded her eyes from the sun. With his basketball spinning on the middle finger of his left hand, Larry glanced up at the top of the Ponderosa pines that bordered the yard. Jeremiah stopped walking but didn't turn around.

"Look," Cody began, "I'm not having a good day—or a good week. I really didn't mean to sound so grouchy."

"It's okay." Feather shrugged. "Everyone has a bad day. Even Mr. Nice."

"Yeah, we've never seen Cody Wayne on an off day," Larry added.

"I don't want you to go," Cody mumbled.

"What did he say?" Jeremiah called out, still not turning around.

"He wants us to stay," Larry informed him.

"Did he say please?"

Cody sighed deeply. "Please," he murmured.

"He said please," Feather called out.

"I'll stay." Jeremiah spun around, a wide, toothy grin on his face.

All three began to mosey back to the porch where Cody stood.

"Cody's right about one thing. We're getting in a rut," Feather admitted.

"So what do we do about it?" Larry quizzed.

Feather clapped her hands. "I have an idea. Each one of us think of something we can do as a group that we haven't done before. Then we write the ideas on slips of paper and put them in a hat. We have to draw one out and then do it."

"Where does she get ideas like this?" Jeremiah pressed.

"Sounds good to me," Cody maintained. "It can't be the same old things, right?"

"Yeah. No practice, powwows, roping, or Risk," Feather insisted.

"And we all have to do it, right?" Larry probed.

"As long as it isn't illegal, immoral, or unbiblical," Cody replied.

"That eliminates all the fun things!" Jeremiah groaned. Then he added, "Just kidding!"

Cody scampered into the house and emerged with pencils and sheets of paper for each.

"Hey, guys." Feather scrunched up her nose and stared down at the blank piece of paper. "I want to consider this a little."

"Yeah, I can't think of anything besides basketball practice." Larry nodded.

"How about us thinking about it and then getting back together after tonight's game?" Feather suggested.

"Yeah . . . sure." Cody shrugged.

"Great! So I think we ought to go to the Treat and Eat and have a soda," Jeremiah announced.

"Is that your activity?" Feather teased.

"No way. I already have mine thought up. I just figure it's time to hit the cafe again."

"I said I was never going back after Feather embarrassed us with Lanni," Cody warned.

"That was a month ago," Larry reminded him.

"It seems like only yesterday to me," Jeremiah said dramatically.

Larry raised his eyebrows. "I know what you mean!"

Feather wrapped her fingers around her neck. "Oh, gag! No swooning over Lanni DeLira!"

"What do you say, cowboy?" Jeremiah teased. "Is the coast clear to head to the cafe?"

"If you three promise not to do anything stupid," Cody cautioned.

Jeremiah shook his head. "You mean I can't blow Mountain Dew out of a straw in my nose?"

"And I can't catapult the butter until it sticks on the ceiling?" Larry prodded.

"I suppose this means you don't want me to write my name on the counter with the mustard squeeze bottle?" Feather sighed.

"Oh, no, you guys can do things like that. I just don't want you to embarrass me. Come on, we'll sit by the door." Cody motioned. "The first gross thing, and I'm out of there."

"Anyone have any money?" Jeremiah asked.

Cody stared at the other three. "Oh, all right, I'm buyin'!"

Still wearing their tie-dyed uniforms, the Lewis and Clark Squad headed for Larry's house to celebrate the victory.

"Did you see that fade-away at the top of the key?" Larry boasted. "It might have been one of the finest shots in my long and memorable career. When the pressure's on, it's Larry Bird Lewis who tosses in the final point!" He carried his basketball in one hand and a gear bag in the other.

"What pressure?" Jeremiah heckled. "We beat them 20 to 6."

"But it was a hard-fought win," Larry maintained.

"They couldn't dribble, pass, or shoot worth squat," Feather reminded him. "What do you mean, hard-fought?"

"I had to work hard not to doze off," Larry joshed.

"The Bobs were just having an off night," Cody defended. "They're better than that."

Feather wore her gray terry cloth towel over her head like a scarf. "Cody thinks every team we beat is just having a bad night. We are pretty good, cowboy. I still can't believe there is a team with three guys named Bob."

"Hey, wouldn't that be a great game to call on the radio?" Larry laughed. He held his nose with pinched fingers and imitated an announcer. "Bob tosses the ball into Bob, who dribbles down across the half-court line and bounce-passes it into Bob, playing post. He fakes a jumper and dumps the ball back out to Bob. The crowd's going wild! But there's only six seconds left. Bob's being double-teamed, and he tosses it across court to Bob, wide open for three! He squares himself at the basket, fires the three . . . 5, 4, 3. It clanged iron! Bob missed the shot! But from out of nowhere, Bob flies in from the foul line, catches the rebound in the air, and slams it home at the buzzer! The Bobs win it! The Bobs win it!"

Jeremiah pinched his nostrils shut and intoned, "The Barfo Cola Player-of-the-Game is . . . Bob! Let's go down to Robert Roberts, who is standing by with Bob." He pointed to Cody.

Cody cupped his hands like a miniature megaphone

and spoke in a deep voice. "Bob, tell me, was that the way you drew up the plan during that last time-out?"

Larry scooted over by Cody and continued the interview. "Yes, in the huddle, Coach Robb said, 'Bob, I want you to take the last shot.'"

Cody cleared his throat. "So when Bob tossed the ball over to Bob, and he bounced it in to Bob, who brought it back out to Bob, who fired it over to Bob for the three-pointer, it was part of the play?"

"Precisely. And my part was to be up in the air when Bob shot, just in case there was a need to put the ball back."

"Well, congratulations again, Bob."

"Thanks," Larry giggled, "but I couldn't have done it without the great playing of Bob, Bob, Bob, and Bob."

"What about the bench?" Jeremiah queried. "They had a good night, right?"

Larry nodded his head. "You're right on that. We had excellent support from our bench, especially Bob and Bob. Even at the end of the third quarter when coach sent in Bob, who was out most of the year with—"

"An amputated leg!" Jeremiah shrieked.

"Yes, well, when he fired in that three-pointer from the half-court line, it showed he's not just any ordinary Bob!"

"You guys have a really, really weird sense of humor!" Feather griped.

"Thank you." Larry bowed. "Thank you very much!"

When they reached Larry's basement den, they

dragged out a huge bag of potato chips and a six-pack of Cokes. They flopped down on the forest-green carpet.

"It's time to pass the hat," Feather informed them. "Larry, get us some pencils and paper. We get to write down something that will get us out of this boring summer rut Cody says we're in."

"I didn't say—"

"I'm teasing you, cowboy! I think this is a great idea— even if it was *my* idea."

"I like it, too," Jeremiah chimed in. "How are we going to do this? Who gets to draw?"

"Me, of course," Feather proclaimed.

"Why you?"

"I'm the only girl."

"Isn't that a sexist statement?" Larry asked.

She stuck out her tongue. "Of course it is. But after centuries of male oppression, I'm allowed to say that!" She looked around at the boys. "That sounded snotty, didn't it?"

"It's okay." Jeremiah shrugged. "We think you ought to draw, too."

"Why?"

"'Cause you're the only girl." He beamed.

"Well," she continued, "I think the first one drawn should be the fourth activity, and we work our way up to number one."

"Sort of a countdown?" Larry asked.

"Yeah. Now everyone fold your papers in half, and then in half again so they'll be the same," Feather instructed.

"That's cool. Here's mine." Larry dropped his into a

University of Indiana baseball cap. "We didn't need to sign our names, did we?"

Feather passed the cap to the others. "I have a feeling we'll all know exactly who wrote what. Okay," she announced, "here's the fourth-place winner."

Larry rolled over to an end table and retrieved his Indiana Pacers cap. He jammed it on his blond hair, bill back. "You mean, here's the loser."

"We are going to do all four activities, so there are no losers." She cleared her throat and stood tall in the middle of the room. "Our fourth activity is: 'Go to Kamiah Basketball Camp for a week and enter as a team.'"

All the eyes focused on Larry.

"Does that sound great, or what?"

They continued to stare.

"It's not just practicing at my house. This is different. There'll be other activities and—"

"I couldn't go with you guys," Feather announced.

"Why?"

"I'm a girl."

"So what? You're with us now," Larry asserted.

"Yeah, well, Kamiah has girls' camps and boys' camps. They don't let you mix them together."

"But you're in a boys' summer league here," Larry persisted.

Feather shook her head. "It won't work, guys. Not everyone is so, eh . . . tolerant."

"Hey, I've got another idea."

"Not basketball, Larry," Cody protested.

"Okay. It's not. Let me write it down."

"Just tell us," Cody urged.

"No, that's not official!" He scribbled a few words on a piece of paper, folded it in the middle, then folded it again, and handed it to Feather.

"And now the revised fourth place goes to: 'We should inner-tube on the Clearwater River.'"

"Whoa, good idea, L. B.!" Jeremiah yelled. "That'll be fun."

"Thank you very much. And you didn't think I could think of anything except basketball."

"We were wrong," Cody admitted.

"Yeah, and if we end up at Canoe Park, we could—"

"Shoot a few buckets?" Cody rolled his eyes.

"Oh, do they have hoops there?"

"I think we've been set up," Jeremiah snorted. "But that's okay. It sounds like a good idea to me. As long as we wait for the water to drop in the river. We'll have to do that one toward the end of summer."

"Now, for the third place . . ." She slowly unfolded the paper. "We are going to ride down Cemetery Grade and have a barbecue with Mr. Levine."

"Hey, that's great!" Cody cheered. "Of course last time we were there, it was kind of dangerous."

"But it wasn't boring," Feather reminded him. "Since this is my idea, I'll get ahold of Mr. Levine and work out the details."

"Do we have to ride bikes home? That grade is a killer!" Jeremiah protested.

"Maybe he'll let us spend the night," Feather suggested.

"Sounds good to me. I hope it's clear at night so we can use his humongous telescope," Larry said. "Now . . . who's the runner-up?"

"Excitement is building," Feather proclaimed. "This is getting to the moment we have been waiting for. In a matter of seconds, the number two activity will be decided. Feather Trailer-Hobbs, the lovely and talented host of this evening's gala event, slowly opens the paper. Now she glances up and coyly announces: 'Finishing in second place is . . . Bob!'"

"Bob?" the boys asked in unison.

"You didn't think you guys had a monopoly on silly commentary, did you?"

"Read the paper!" Jeremiah insisted.

"It says: 'We should camp out on Arrowhead Butte Monday and see what gets released.'"

"All right!" Jeremiah shouted. "Mine's number one! There is justice for the red man!"

"Just a minute," she insisted. "We're not through with number two, which must be Cody's suggestion. He says: 'I figure we can keep out of sight and see what turns up. At least we can play some games while we wait.'"

"What if my mom won't let me spend the day in the woods with three boys?"

"We'll do something different. We aren't going to do it without you," Cody insisted.

Feather's green eyes stared straight at Cody. "You're serious, aren't you?"

"You're on the Squad, Feather-girl," Larry assured her. "We stick together."

"Okay, Monday we go to Arrowhead Butte," she agreed. "Now for the number one selection . . ."

"I'd just like to say that in accepting this honor," Jeremiah began, "I am fulfilling a lifelong dream. I'd like to thank everyone who made this possible, especially the little people who supported me all along. And I'd like to thank my fellow contestants who gave me a real challenge."

"Sit down, Townie!" Cody hooted.

"And finally I'd like to thank DeVonne."

"Why?" Cody asked.

"Just in case she's out there watching this."

"Out where?"

Feather peeked out the high window. "In Larry's front yard?"

"Out there in televisionland. Surely this event is being televised on ESPN," Jeremiah jibed.

"Read the blinking note!" Larry growled.

"Our first activity is: 'Hike up Travois Grade, across the trestles, and through the tunnel at Deception Pass!'"

"No!" Cody protested. "No, we aren't!"

"Come on, toughest man in Halt. It will be a hoot, and you know it," Jeremiah challenged.

Cody flung himself back on the carpet. *I can't do it, Lord. . . . I just can't do it!*

"Speaking of Halt," Feather continued, "do you guys know how Halt got its name?"

Cody stared up at the brass light fixture. *Lord, there are two things I can't do this summer—fight J. J. and hike through the tunnel at Deception Pass. Maybe some other year.*

"Oh, no!" Larry groaned. "Not another wild story about Halt!"

"It's not wild. This is the truth. One of the first settlers in the region was a man whose last name was Solomon."

"She's right about that," Jeremiah put in. "The Solomons used to live out on Powerline Road. Right, Cody?"

Cody clasped his hands behind his head. *Lord, what if You're trying to tell me to stay away from Deception Pass? You used dreams to speak to people in the Bible. If I go up there, I might be testing You. That wouldn't be right . . . would it?*

"Anyway," she continued, "Mr. Solomon had four daughters. Their names were Harriet, Adele, Louisa, and Thelma."

"Thelma?"

"Yes, and he couldn't decide which one to name the town after."

On the other hand, Lord, I know that sometimes Satan tries to make us afraid of things we shouldn't be afraid of. Deception Pass didn't used to bother me at all. Cody wiped sweat off his forehead.

"So he chose the first letter of each of their names!" Jeremiah hollered.

"Exactly." Feather danced in a circle.

Cody rolled over on his side and propped himself up on his elbow. *Well, I'm just not going to do it. There's no reason to take a chance. Not one good reason.*

"Why didn't he call the place Lath, Thal, or Athl?" Larry chuckled.

"Because he used the names chronologically."

"What do you think, Cody?" Jeremiah asked.

"Cody?" Larry pressed.

"No!" he blurted out. "It's not right!"

"I was just pretending," Feather explained. "Everyone else gets to make up stories about Halt's name."

"Are we on the same page, cowboy?" Jeremiah asked. "We're talking about how Halt got its name."

Cody glanced around at the others. "Huh?"

Jeremiah pointed a potato chip at him. "That's what I thought. He's off in la-la land."

"Look, guys, this thing about Deception Pass," Cody implored. "I've had some bad dreams about it. I don't think we should do it."

"Doo-doo-doo-doo, doo-doo-doo-doo . . ." Jeremiah pinched his broad brown nose. "You are now entering the Twilight Zone."

"The best way to overcome a fear is to meet it head on," Larry announced.

"Where did you hear that?" Feather questioned.

"In an article by Bobby Knight about how to beat a team that has an obvious height advantage," Larry admitted. "But the principle holds."

"Cody, you can come along, and then if there's some part of it you don't want to do, you can bale out," Feather suggested.

"No, it's deeper than that," Cody argued. "You don't understand!"

"I understand a cowboy keeps his word, and we all promised to do whatever the others suggested," Feather lectured.

"But I didn't know Townie would—"

"Hey," Jeremiah interrupted, "I guess I could change it. What do you want us to do, Cody?"

"I can't decide for you."

"You just did," Larry pointed out.

"What do you mean?"

"You shot down Townie's idea, forcing him to think of another. That's deciding for him, isn't it?"

"It is?"

"Sure." Larry plucked the bag of chips from Jeremiah's hand and crammed several into his mouth.

Cody looked each of them in the eyes. "Oh, man, I'm going to regret this. Okay . . . we're going to hike over Deception Pass, but you said I have the right to turn back if I need to."

"Hey, we all have the right to bale out if we need to—right, guys?" Feather asked.

"I'm a brave warrior," Jeremiah declared, "but not stupid."

"What do you say, Cody? Shall we tackle the grade?" Larry proposed.

Cody's heart shouted no, but his head nodded agreement with the others.

Five

I get number four," Jeremiah announced as he plopped down on the rough wooden bench in front of the Buy Rite Market, a root beer in his right hand. His black butch haircut glistened with sweat.

Larry dribbled over to the bench and sprawled next to Cody. "You and Cody have three and four. I might as well take five. Did I ever tell you guys it was my lucky number?"

Cody took a big swig of his Mountain Dew. His back ached, his hand felt raw, and his thigh muscles burned under the Wranglers. He glanced at Larry. "We knew about your lucky lasagna, lucky brownies, lucky meat loaf, lucky lemon pie, lucky fudge, and even your lucky tuna-and-black-olive sandwich, but I've never heard about your lucky five." He peered at Jeremiah with raised eyebrows. "You know, Townie, this might be one of the two or three best Mountain Dews I've had in my entire life."

"A 9+?" Jeremiah quizzed.

"Perhaps a 10-," Cody asserted.

"You guys rate each Dew?"

Jeremiah tossed up his hands in disbelief. "Don't you?"

"They all taste the same to me."

"Yeah, and I suppose all cows look alike to you," Cody teased.

"Eh . . . yeah."

"Hey, here comes Cody's rig! You get Mr. Stillwell's old IH pickup!"

"Where's the top of the cab?" Larry asked.

"He rolled it one night thirty years ago, so he took the torch and cut the top off."

Larry stopped dribbling and balanced the basketball on top of his head. "You mean it looks that way on purpose?"

"Yeah," Cody replied. "Kind of rough, isn't it?"

They watched the rig smoke and chug down the highway.

"It looks like what's left after a bomb goes off." Larry tilted his head back, catching the ball between his neck and the front of the store.

"It looks better now than it does during a snowstorm in January," Cody remarked. "Does this mean I don't win?"

"An old bicycle would beat that. Take a good look, boys, because here comes a winner! Mine is a like-new Toyota Forerunner," Jeremiah bragged. "What can I say? If you've got it, you've got it. I got it."

Cody pointed down the highway. "Here comes Larry's."

"A motorcycle?" Larry croaked. "Do we count motorcycles?"

"Yep," Cody smirked.

"Well, it's a nice motorcycle," Larry observed. "Look at all that chrome! And what about those studded black leather saddlebags? Does my hog win?"

"Nope." Cody reached over and jabbed the basketball out from behind Larry's neck. "It's not a Harley-Davidson; it's a Kawasaki."

Jeremiah grabbed the ball and threw up a hook shot that landed on Cody's lap. "Either way it doesn't beat a late-model Forerunner."

Larry retrieved his basketball and bent forward to dribble. The other two leaned back against the front of the Buy Rite Market and watched the Sunday afternoon traffic on the Highway 95 bypass.

Jeremiah tried to look serious. "Well, boys, it jist don't git no better than this!"

"Playing Cool Rig on an Idaho early August summer day is the ultimate?" Larry questioned. "What about the NBA championship? What about NCAA play-offs? What about the three-on-three Youth Summer League championship game?"

"After working almost all week loading hay, this seems nicer," Cody admitted.

"You're weird, Clark."

"Thank you. Thank you very much. What direction are we on?"

"West. And here comes the third car."

"No! No! I can't believe it!" Cody groaned. "I didn't think that old truck still ran. It's been parked out in front of Mr. Robinson's for ten years."

"Well, it's running today, Cody Wayne. Hey, don't

sweat it," Jeremiah insisted. "Look at what I've got coming down the road. You couldn't have won no matter what. Turn out the lights; let the fat lady sing; that, my boys, is a '96 metallic red Mustang convertible with a blonde goddess driving it! Am I on a roll, or what? That is gorgeous!"

"The car or the blonde?" Cody teased.

"Both!"

"I've got the next one," Larry called. "Hey, that's no fair. It's the guy on the motorcycle again." Larry spun his Indiana Pacers cap backwards. "I don't think I should have to have the same rig."

"I've got a shutout going—2 to 0 to 0!" Jeremiah bragged. "You know, I just might be the Michael Jordan of Cool Rig."

Larry stared off toward the north. "What kind of car does Feather's dad drive?" he asked.

"An old VW bug," Cody reported. "Why?"

"I saw a VW bus turn down Second Street. I thought maybe it was him." Larry stuck his legs straight out from the bench and dribbled the ball back and forth under them.

"It's too bad she had to go with her dad today. I was all set to hike over Deception Pass," Jeremiah said.

Cody pushed his hat to the back of his head. *Thank You, Lord.*

"Maybe Grandpa will let us use his new video camera. We'll have it all on tape. We could send it to that funniest home video program."

"Yeah, but something weird would have to happen.

Anyway, Tuesday sounds good to me," Larry proclaimed. "Provided we survive the ordeal on Arrowhead Butte."

Cody glanced down at the toes of his brown boots. *Now if You could make it rain on Tuesday.*

"Why do you think Feather's dad wanted her to go to Lewiston with him?" Jeremiah asked. "She's hardly seen him more than once in the past three months."

"Maybe he loves her," Cody suggested. "She *is* his only daughter."

"Yeah, I guess." Larry glanced toward the old, worn swinging screen door of the market and then lowered his voice. "But I'm with Townie. Dumping Feather and her mother down here while he lives with some other gal doesn't sound like he loves them much."

"I have a hard time figuring out other kids," Cody admitted. "There's no way I can understand someone else's parents."

"Here comes Larry's buddy!" Jeremiah chuckled.

"The guy on the motorcycle?" Larry croaked. "Hey, it's not my turn. That's your rig this time, Cody."

Cody shook his head. "Well, he's the only guy from out of state I've ever known to cruise Halt." He tossed his empty Mountain Dew can toward a blue recycling container. "Ah hah! Nothing but . . . plastic!"

"Out of state?" Larry queried. "How can you read that little license plate?"

"He's from Arizona," Cody declared. "That burgundy plate is Arizona. Only don't get that confused with Missouri."

"Well, wherever he's from, he hasn't helped anyone win a game yet!" Larry sighed. "The traffic's slow today."

"The traffic is slow every day," Cody laughed.

The voice was high-pitched, nervous, urgent. "Hey, Cody!"

All three boys craned their necks to the east toward the sprawling cottonwood tree that separated the dirt parking lot of the market from the vine-covered chain-link fence of Earl's Equipment Rental and Videos.

"Timmy, is that you? Are you in the tree?" Cody called out.

"Yeah, come here!"

Cody, Larry, and Jeremiah strolled toward the cottonwood. Its lower light green leafy branches almost drooped to the ground. "You need help getting down?"

"No! I'm hiding. Don't look up here! Pretend like you're just talking to each other."

Cody stepped into the shade of the tree and spotted the suntanned, shirtless, shoeless ten-year-old clinging to a limb about six feet from the ground. His blond hair was uncombed, and a smear of mud or chocolate or both ran from his ear to his chin.

Cody turned his back to the tree and stared out at the highway. "Timmy, what's going on?"

"J. J. knows you're at the store. He's coming over to challenge you to a fight."

"When?"

"Right now. I was at the park and heard him and Rocky get into an argument."

Cody shifted his weight from one boot to the other. "What about?"

"Rocky said he thought the idea of fighting you was dumb, and he didn't want any part of it. J. J. called him some names. I thought they were going to fight it out right there, but Rocky just went home."

"Was Devin with them?" Cody rubbed the back of his neck. It felt sunburned.

"Yeah. He said he'd give J. J. a ride over here, but he wasn't going to help him fight. If they find out I've squealed, I'm history."

Larry glanced back over his shoulder at the boy in the tree. "They won't do anything to you."

"Last time I turned them in, they ran over my bicycle. I don't have any more bicycles."

For the first time all day the summer air tasted stale. "Okay, go on, Timmy. You warned me."

"Can I stay up here and watch the fight?"

"There's not going to be a fight," Cody contended.

"Can I stay up here and watch the not-a-fight?"

"Sure."

"Thanks, Cody. Listen, no matter what happens, I think you're the toughest kid in town. I've been telling everybody that."

"You're the one that got that started?" Cody quizzed.

"Yep. But you don't have to thank me. It's true. You are the toughest."

Cody, Larry, and Jeremiah dogged it back across the parking lot toward the bench in front of the market.

"What are we going to do?" Jeremiah asked.

"We?" Larry croaked.

"Larry's right. It's my deal, Townie."

"Well, then, what are *you* going to do?"

"Try to talk him out of it again."

"And if that doesn't work?"

"Try to keep from getting pounded into the gravel."

"We could slip down the alley and head for my house," Jeremiah suggested.

Cody shook his head. "I'm not going to run."

"Why not? Cool Rig is getting predictable. You aren't running. You're just going home."

Cody dropped his elbows to his knees and held his head in his hands. "Down the alley?"

"Who would know?" Larry quizzed.

"Timmy," Cody replied. "And after that, every kid in town."

"So what?" Larry tucked the basketball under his arm. "You too proud to keep from getting pounded?"

"Nope. It's just . . . well, kids like Timmy get picked on all the time. He knows how to run. But I don't know if he knows how to stand."

"Let his dad teach him," Larry insisted.

Cody lowered his voice to a whisper. "Timmy's dad was killed in that train wreck in the snow up on Deception Pass a few years ago."

Larry huddled closer. "Wow, did he fall off one of those trestles?"

"He got caught between two cars."

Larry's mouth dropped open.

Jeremiah squatted down on top of the bench. "So we're going to wait it out?"

"I guess."

"Hey, look!" Larry pointed to the west side of the market. "Mr. Arizona Kawasaki is at Buy Rite! I vote we eliminate him from future competition."

"Are you two ready to play again?" Cody grilled.

"Are you sure it's a good idea just to wait for J. J.?" Larry asked.

"I think so." Cody rapped his fingertips on the knees of his Wranglers. *Maybe Townie is right. I should run home down the alley. I don't need to sit here like a duck on a pond. We could go into the store, look around, and cut out the side door on the alley. Timmy wouldn't see me run.*

Lord, why am I so concerned with how I look to Timmy?

How do I look to You, Lord?

Okay, I look like a scared kid.

A noise from inside the store caused all three boys to turn to the screen door.

"Sounds like someone dropped something!" Cody said in alarm.

"Someone's yelling. Who's working today?" Jeremiah questioned.

Seated closest to the door, Cody stood. "Just Mr. Addney and Feather's mom. Maybe she needs some help." He scurried to the door.

"Well, hurry!" Jeremiah shouted. "Here comes J. J. Go on! Get in there!"

Cody jumped forward when he spotted the yellow

Jeep. As he did, he heard someone inside holler, "Cody, look out!"

Man, why is everyone—

The toe of his boot crashed into the screen door. It swung inward like the crack of a whip, slamming into the hands and chin of the exiting biker. He staggered back inside, dropping his packages.

Now this guy will want to punch my lights out, too!

Cody hurried inside and scooped up the brown paper sack and the metal object lying beside it.

A 9mm semiautomatic pistol?

Cody picked up the weapon and the sack and stared at the man in black leather struggling to his feet. Tight lines were drawn across the man's face, especially around his eyes.

"Give me my gun, kid!"

"Cody, he robbed the store!" Mrs. Trailer-Hobbs cried out.

"You won't shoot me, kid. You can't!" the man snarled.

Facing Cody, with his back to the checkout stand, the thief never saw the twelve-pack of diet creme sodas Feather's mother slammed into his head. He wobbled wildly toward Cody in a desperate dive for the gun. Cody pulled the gun up and away from his side. The barrel of the pistol accidentally cracked into the man's chin, and the thief crashed into the concrete floor. Larry and Townie peered in through the doorway.

"Whoa! You coldcocked him, Cody Wayne!"

"All right!" Larry whooped.

Cody could hear Feather's mother crying behind him.

He still held the paper sack in one hand and the gun in the other.

"Are y-you all right?" he stammered.

"Just scared, Mr. Nice. . . . Keep that gun pointed on that creep while I call the sheriff."

"Yes, ma'am." With his hand on the cold black metal trigger, Cody stood above the motionless man.

I'm not scared. I'm not going to cry. Lord, if he moves, You know there's no way I could pull this trigger. I'm not scared. Well, maybe just a little.

Yeah, right.

Mrs. Trailer-Hobbs fumbled with the black dial phone. "Jeremiah?"

"Yes, ma'am?"

"Run over to the cafe and get Mr. Addney. He just went to eat."

"Larry, get some clothesline rope down on aisle two and tie that guy up."

"But I don't tie very well and—"

"Get the rope. Mr. Nice can tie him."

Larry raced down the grocery store aisle as Mrs. Trailer-Hobbs told the county sheriff's dispatcher the situation. Cody squatted down next to the man, holding the gun only inches above the man's head.

Lord, keep him down. I don't care if he doesn't wake up for three days. I'm not going to shake. I'm not going to cry.

Cody was startled when the swinging screen door swung open. When he lifted his head to look, he lifted the pistol as well.

"Clark!" J. J. shouted. "You can't hide in . . ." His eyes

froze on the unconscious man and the gun in Cody's hand. "Oh, crud!" J. J. gulped. "I'm leaving!"

"He, eh, tried to . . . get away," Cody explained.

"I'm out of here!" J. J. cried. He flung the door open and dove into the dirt and gravel parking lot.

Cody heard the Jeep roar out of the lot. Larry handed him a package of rope. He handed Larry the paper sack and gun and began to tie up the unconscious man.

"This sack is full of money!" Larry croaked.

Footsteps sounded at the door, and Mr. Addney raced in with an Idaho State Patrolman, who took over from Cody. The boys huddled next to the checkout counter. Mrs. Trailer-Hobbs scooted up to Cody and put her arm around his shoulder.

"Thanks, Cody Wayne!" She smiled. "But I yelled at you to run, not drop the guy."

"I, eh . . . got kind of excited and confused."

"The reluctant hero," she proclaimed.

"There's nothing heroic about being scared spitless," he mumbled.

"And there's nothing cowardly about being scared. Especially when the guy has a loaded gun," Mrs. Trailer-Hobbs consoled.

"It wasn't loaded," the trooper called out after hand-cuffing the groggy thief.

"What?" Jeremiah choked.

"He didn't even have the clip in it, and there's nothing in the chamber," the uniformed officer explained.

"Why pull a robbery with a gun if it's not loaded?" Jeremiah asked.

"Scared of shooting someone, I suppose," the patrolman replied.

"I certainly didn't know it wasn't loaded," Mrs. Trailer-Hobbs admitted.

"Me either," Cody gulped. "No wonder he came right after me."

"It's a good thing you coldcocked him. He might have hurt you," the patrolman warned.

"Oh, man," Cody sighed. "I didn't really do anything. It's just—"

"Boys, you go back there and help yourself to some cookies and sodas. I'm buying," Mr. Addney offered. "The sheriff will want to talk to you when he gets here. You saved me some major dollars today!"

They ate.

Drank.

Told their story.

Several times.

To the patrolman.

To the sheriff.

To a newspaper reporter.

To Cody's mother over the phone.

And finally to Timmy Jorgenson.

"You should have seen J. J. dive into the dirt," Timmy whooped. "I thought maybe you had slugged him. He rolled all the way from the door to the car. It was totally awesome."

"He just got scared and ran off," Cody tried to explain.

"Rolled off, you mean!" Jeremiah snickered.

"But you didn't run or roll. You stayed right there and caught the crook," Timmy insisted.

"I was too scared to run off."

"Wait until I tell the others that J. J.'s afraid of you!" Timmy squealed.

"No!" Cody barked. "Don't tell them that! You told them enough. J. J. did the right thing. It's smart to be scared of a man with a gun."

"Well, I can tell my mom, can't I?" Timmy sprinted barefoot down the gravel and dirt street.

"That kid has feet of steel," Larry marveled.

"Pound for pound, Timmy's probably the toughest kid in town," Cody added.

"I think I'll go tell my mom, too," Jeremiah reported.

"Then you have to come to my house," Cody insisted. "My mom will want to hear your side of things, too."

Cody told the entire account once again to his mother. Then to his father and Denver.

Later on to Prescott and Reno when they called.

After that Larry and Jeremiah spent half an hour at Cody's house giving their version. They left for home about dark.

At 9:15 P.M. Feather knocked on Cody's front door.

"Feather! How's your dad?"

She tilted her head to the side and rested it on her right index finger. "Let's see—he loves me but doesn't want to live with me or have me live with him. He respects my mom but can't live with her either. He's having a wonderful summer with his girlfriend. They spent most of last week chained to a Forest Service bulldozer. And he's so broke he's going to sell the tepee and the property north of town. He bought me a $1.99 veggie burger and said he'd see me in September. But that's not why I'm here, and you know it."

Cody jammed his thumbs into the belt loops of his Wranglers and stared down at the concrete porch. "I guess you heard what happened."

"I heard and I'm mad!" she pouted. Her extremely long brown hair was combed out full.

Cody thought about telling her how nice it looked that way.

But he didn't.

Instead, he stepped outside on the porch and closed the door behind him. "Why are you mad?"

"Because you weren't supposed to do anything exciting until I got back. We're a team. The Lewis and Clark Squad, remember? Of which there are four members."

"We didn't plan on doing anything. It was just a dull, lazy Sunday afternoon. How were we to know that someone would try to rob Buy Rite? Mr. Addney said no one's tried that since 1968."

"Oh, I know, cowboy. Mom told me everything about it."

Feather wore cut-off jeans shorts and a pink blouse with lacy short sleeves. She strolled over to the iron and oak bench in the middle of Cody's covered porch and sat, folding her long, thin legs underneath her.

"Your mom's the one who clobbered the robber with

the soda. He stumbled into me, and the floor sort of finished him off."

"That's not exactly the way she tells it." Feather rolled her green eyes to the porch roof and then tilted her head toward Cody. "She said that when she yelled, you came running to help her, even though the guy had a gun in his hand."

Cody sat down on the opposite end of the wooden bench. "Actually, I didn't know that—"

"She said you were the first male of any age who put her safety above his own. She cried when she told me that, Cody. My mom doesn't cry much anymore. You know that."

Cody stared out into the north-central Idaho darkness. Above the trees he could see the first sign of stars blinking on. A pleasant, cool breeze filtered through the second growth Ponderosa pines. "I guess, maybe, I was just where the Lord wanted me to be."

Feather rubbed both of her earlobes at the same time. "That's what I told my mother."

"You did? What did she say?" Cody noticed the tiny silver chain that connected her double earrings.

"She said if she didn't watch out . . ." She paused and bit her lower lip. "Mr. Nice was going to convert her just like you converted me."

He whipped his head around to face her. "I converted you?"

"Cody Wayne Clark, of course you converted me. Six weeks ago I had no place in my life for God. I didn't believe in Him at all."

He looked down at the slats in the bench. "And now?"

"Just wait. About three weeks ago . . . you know, when we moved to town and all? Well, I wasn't so sure anymore. I kept thinking maybe you were right. Now, well, I know you're right. There's just got to be a God who can make sense out of things."

It was a funny feeling.

A funny, *good* feeling.

It started way at the bottom of Cody's throat and sort of tickled. It seemed as if his spirit was jumping and his body relaxing at the same time. He knew he had a foolish grin on his face. He just didn't care. It felt great.

A sort of funny, *great* feeling.

"You're right, Feather-girl, there is a God who can make sense of it all. Isn't that cool?"

"I'm sure glad, because my life . . . and sometimes my mind is so mixed up. Now before you get the big head and say, 'I told you so,' I want you to know I haven't done that Jesus thing yet. But I probably will one of these days. You know what my problem is? It's you, Cody Wayne."

"Me?"

"If I do this Jesus thing, then I'll have to be Miss Nice. And I don't think I can do that. I've got a really terrible mind sometimes, and if I'm with the wrong crowd, I've got a terrible mouth."

"I've never heard you . . ."

"That's because you're part of the right crowd, cowboy. What am I talking about? I came over here to hear your story of the attempted robbery. How did you get me on this subject anyway?"

Cody shrugged his shoulders. "I don't think I've said three words."

She turned her nose up a little. "Are you bragging or complaining?"

"Neither." Cody took a deep breath of fresh night air. *I don't know what to say. I wish I knew how to talk to girls.* "Is your mom doing all right now?"

"Yeah. Mr. Addney gave her a raise," Feather announced.

"Because of the robbery attempt?"

"Sort of." She traced her fingers over the oak slats of the bench. "He said if he was going to leave her alone like that, she should get more money. Mom figured it would be enough of a raise to pay most of the bills every month."

Cody leaned back on the bench and crammed his hands in the front pockets of his jeans. *You mean, she hasn't had enough money to pay the bills till now?* "I'm glad something good came out of all of this."

"You know what else my mom said?"

"What?"

"She said she likes Mr. Nice and is glad I had enough good sense to become your friend. Yeah, did you know you're the first boy I've ever known that my mother likes?"

"Really?"

"Normally, I try to hang out with jerks," Feather teased. "Did I tell you about the guy I used to like that had a fishhook in his nose?"

Cody shuddered. "On purpose?"

"Yeah. He said it was an antifishing statement or something. It was sterling silver and all. Other than that, he was just your ordinary foul-mouthed jerk. But he wasn't the worst. They've all been jerks."

"Why did you change your style?"

"Halt, Idaho, is so tiny there just aren't enough jerks to go around. I moved here late, and most of the real jerks were already taken."

"So you had to settle for what was left over?"

"What's a girl to do? You got to work with what you've got."

"I can tell you one thing—I've never known anyone on earth like you," Cody admitted.

"I'll bet you haven't. I'm kind of weird, aren't I?"

Cody laughed. "Feather-girl, you are beyond a doubt the weirdest person I ever met."

"Thank you," she giggled. "Thank you very much. Now what do you really mean?"

"I mean, in thirteen years I have never spoken to any girl more than two minutes at a time in my life."

"Never? Not even your mom?"

"Moms don't count as girls."

"Not even to the Honey Del Mateo types?"

"Especially the Honey Del Mateo types! But I can talk to you and not worry about every word sounding dumb or boring or nerdy."

"That's probably because I'm so gracious and charming," she giggled.

Cody stared at her as the light of the living room lamps reflected off her face. *I think she's waiting for me to say something, but I don't have any idea what it is.*

Feather broke the silence by blurting out, "Girls mature more quickly than boys!"

Cody blinked hard. "What does that have to do with anything?"

"I could see it in your eyes."

"You could see what?"

"The lack of maturity!" She scowled.

"What?"

"Oh, nothing, Cody Wayne! You take everything too seriously." She scooted over toward him on the bench.

He tried to move back but pinned himself against the black iron handrail.

"Relax, cowboy. I want you to tell me, step by step, every single thing that happened down at Buy Rite Market this afternoon."

"Everything?"

"Yes."

"It all started when I bought a great Mountain Dew . . . and we settled in to play a game of Cool Rig."

She scooted a little closer toward him. "How good was it?"

"The Dew?" Cody wiped the sweat off the back of his neck.

"Yes."

"A 9+."

"Wow! You did have a good day! Keep going. I want to hear the details."

So he told her.

Feather listened intently to every word and, to Cody's relief, didn't move any closer.

Six

*T*here he is, folks—Halt's favorite son!" Jeremiah cheered as Cody strolled out of the house.

"What are you three doing here?"

Larry wore dark glasses and his University of Indiana cap turned backwards. "And so modest! Look, Cody-baby, I told the press I'm your agent. They have to come through me on all endorsements. Spielberg wanted you in a feature film, but I told him we wouldn't settle for anything less than twenty mil and 1 percent of gross."

"This is all gross," Cody retorted.

"Oh, Cody Wayne," Feather folded her hands under her chin and swooned. "Can I have your autograph? Or maybe a lock of your hair! I think I'm going to faint." She fluttered her eyelids.

He pushed his hand toward their silly grins. "I think I'm going to barf."

Jeremiah threw his arm around Cody's shoulder. "You did see your picture in the *Lewiston Examiner*, didn't you?"

Cody nodded. "Yeah, on page 6. I had my eyes closed and looked like a dork."

Jeremiah pointed his finger at Cody. "But a *heroic* dork."

Cody slipped out of Jeremiah's grasp. "Did you see that crummy caption under the photo: 'Diet-Creme Kid Captures Crook'? It was Feather's mom who clobbered the guy. Why did they get it messed up like that?"

"Cody-baby," Larry lectured, "remember, in show biz any publicity is good publicity."

Cody wandered down the steps ahead of the others.

"Hey, Cody, can I be your bodyguard?" Jeremiah asked. "I'll taste all the food for you and check out the babes."

"Okay, you guys, you had your fun." Cody grinned for the first time. "Now what are you really doing over here?"

"How do you like that?" Feather faked a pout. "He invites us over and then pretends he doesn't know anything about it."

"He's probably been busy lining up the *Letterman Show*," Jeremiah suggested.

"Oh, no!" Larry waved his hands. "I handle all the bookings for Cody-baby."

Cody raised his eyebrows in a scowl. "If you say Cody-baby one more time, Lewis, I'll cram those shades up your left nostril!"

"Whoa," Larry rumbled, "he's going to be one of those temperamental brat-pack stars! The tabloids will have a field day with this."

"Remember the trek to Arrowhead Butte?" Feather reminded Cody.

"Arrowhead Butte!" Cody moaned. "I can't believe I forgot about that!"

Larry tugged his dark glasses to the end of his nose and looked over the top of the frames. "Look, the whole reason we're here is to stop someone from releasing something on Arrowhead Butte today, or at least that's what you dreamed."

"It wasn't a dream," Cody insisted. "I really heard it."

"I packed food that should last all day." Feather pointed to an olive green backpack perched on the concrete step. "If someone doesn't eat like a horse."

"Why are all of you looking at me?" Jeremiah questioned. "I've got the drinks!"

"And I've got a complete activity schedule," Larry put in. "Say, is there anyplace to practice on Arrowhead Butte?"

"Absolutely none," Cody reported. "There's absolutely no reason to bring a basketball."

"That's as stupid as saying there's no reason to breathe. Of course, we're bringing a basketball. Anyway, I'm sure we could work on passes."

"All day?" Feather protested.

"We could change off by sprinting up the Butte. It should strengthen our jumping muscles."

"I don't jump," Jeremiah protested. "It's hard on my knees."

Cody quieted the trio. "I'll get Denver to haul us

around to the back of the lake, and we'll hike in from there."

"What if we spend the day back there, and nothing happens?" Jeremiah pressed.

"Then we can check Cody's activity off the list," Feather replied.

Jeremiah strutted in red shorts and tank top, flexing his muscles. "And tomorrow we conquer Deception Pass!"

"If it doesn't rain," Cody added.

"Rain?" Jeremiah responded. "There hasn't been anything close to rain for a couple weeks."

"Then we're due," Cody mumbled. *Lord, tomorrow would really be a good time for a downpour, a real monsoon.*

The north side of Arrowhead Butte was treeless except for one lightning-damaged cedar three-quarters of the way up the Butte. The grassy carpet was plenty deep for a sleeping Cody not to be seen below, but not nearly tall enough to hide four bored members of the Lewis and Clark Squad. Noon found them sprawled in what little shade there was under the lone cedar tree.

"What's in this one?" Jeremiah opened a sandwich.

"That has celery, mushrooms, walnuts, and mayo. It's very crunchy," Feather explained.

"The bread is all seedy."

"That's alfalfa sprout bread. It's very healthy, you know."

"Healthy? It looks like it's growing."

"That one's mine anyway," she informed him. "Yours is down at the bottom of the sack."

"This one?"

"Yeah, the one on plain, unhealthy white bread with nothing but a thick slab of baloney and Grey Poupon mustard."

"Really?" Jeremiah bubbled. "All right! My all-time favorite sandwich!"

"What did you fix for me?" Larry asked.

"Sourdough bread, lettuce, tomato, sweet pickle slices, Swiss cheese, plain mustard, mayonnaise, and a stack of thin sliced turkey," she replied triumphantly.

"Awesome!" Larry hooted. "My favorite. I think I'm in love!"

"With Feather?" Jeremiah mocked.

"No, with this sandwich! What did you get, Cody?"

"I made Cody unsalted peanut butter and jalapeño peppers on rye bread with blue cheese dressing," she declared.

Cody stared at the sandwich now resting in his hand. *This is a joke. She's teasing me, right?*

"That looks totally disgusting, cowboy," Larry groaned. "I can't believe you like that!"

"Well, actually—" Cody began.

"No one should complain now. Everyone has his favorite."

Cody continued to stare at the sticky sandwich in front of him.

"Go ahead and dig in, guys. Don't worry, I made each of you two sandwiches!"

Two of these? She's serious! I'm supposed to eat this? Favorite? Oh, man . . . what am I going to do? There's been a major mistake here.

Cody popped open a bag of Fritos and tossed a couple into his mouth.

"Mmphth wdw, msser novcb." Jeremiah swallowed and repeated himself, "How did you find out what our favorite sandwiches are?"

"I called your mothers last night," Feather explained.

My mother did this to me? I always thought she liked me.

"'Course I couldn't get ahold of Cody's mom. Their phone was tied up last night. But I saw Denver and Becky sitting in his pickup over at the park, so I banged on the window and asked him."

"You asked Denver?" Cody fumed.

"Yeah, it was after dark. I think I startled them a little."

Denver! He did this to me? I'll . . . I'll think of something!

"It *is* your favorite sandwich, isn't it, Cody?" she asked.

"Eh . . ." He glanced over at Feather's eager face. "Well, not exactly."

"What is your favorite?"

"Roast beef and catsup on sourdough."

"Is this your second favorite?"

Cody stared down the slope of Arrowhead Butte. "Eh, no, a cold meat loaf sandwich would probably be my second."

Feather lifted her chin. "Just where would you put this one?"

I'd like to cram it down Denver's throat!

"Cody, where does this one rank?"

"You want me to be honest?" he said.

"Sure."

"Dead last."

"What?"

"I can't imagine ever in my life eating something like that."

Feather bit her lip, and Cody noticed tears coming in her eyes.

"Hey, it's okay," he consoled her. "I'm not very hungry really. I think Denver was playing a trick on you—well, at least, on me."

Feather crossed her arms and held them tight against her chest. "Why would he do that?"

"It might have something to do with your sneaking up on him and Becky," Larry proposed.

"I didn't sneak." A grin spread across Feather's freckled face. "Well, maybe I walked real quietly!" She held out a sandwich to Cody. "I'll share mine with you."

"Eh, no, thanks. Really, I'll just eat some chips and . . ." He dug through the canvas backpack. " . . . a carrot."

The sun was directly above the cedar. The only shade was straight beneath its drooping branches. All four members of the Lewis and Clark Squad sprawled on their backs in the wild grass to watch several mounds of white clouds sail toward them from the west.

Feather waved a long, thin arm toward the sky. "Look

at that second one. Doesn't it look just like a sailboat with its sail in the wind?"

Larry lay on his back and tossed the basketball high above the grass and then caught it. "The second one? Nah, man . . . it looks just like a brand-new basketball net—a thick nylon net that jumps and pops when a long, arcing shot hits it from behind the three-point line."

"Are we talking about the same cloud?" Feather asked.

"That second one, right?"

"What about it, Townie? What's it look like to you?" she probed.

"Like a side order of mashed potatoes just waiting for dark brown gravy," Jeremiah replied.

"What do you think, Cody?" Feather asked.

"Say, is it just me," Cody chuckled, "or does it look like a . . ."

"A what?"

"A white cloud floating across a blue sky?"

"That's what I would expect from His Slugness," she said scornfully.

"His what?" Larry inquired.

"Cody has the imagination of a slug."

"Thank you," Cody snickered. "Thank you very much."

"We aren't really going to lie here all afternoon, are we?" Larry asked. "I don't know about you guys, but I'm getting really bored."

"Let's go down in the trees and play tag or something," Jeremiah proposed.

"We could run some drills," Larry suggested.

Feather jumped up, grabbed Larry's basketball, and flung it down the north slope of Arrowhead Butte.

"What did you do that for?" Larry hollered. "I could lose my favorite wilderness basketball!"

"Let's play Capture the Spalding!" she shouted. "First one to the ball wins!" She ran several steps down the slope. Larry and Jeremiah flew past her. Feather stopped and looked back at Cody. "I knew you wouldn't run."

"Well, we ought to clean things up here and—"

"And you're afraid we'll scare off the people who are going to release . . . radioactive isotopes or whatever."

Cody started cramming trash into a small brown paper sack. "That's not it."

"You just don't like jumping and running because a girl tells you to jump and run?"

Cody didn't say anything but kept sacking things up.

"That's it, isn't it, Cody Wayne?" Feather maintained.

"Sort of," he mumbled.

"Sort of?" she pressed.

"Yeah, I don't do well when I think someone's trying to control me."

"Well, Cody Wayne." She held the hem of her jeans shorts and curtsied. "Would you like to join your team-mates in a game of Capture the Spalding?"

Cody reached up and tipped his straw cowboy hat at her. "Yes, ma'am, I would."

"Oh, brother," she mumbled. "Cody, sometimes when I'm with you, I get the feeling I'm in the last century."

"Thank you." He flashed his less-than-straight-toothed grin. "Thank you very much."

Capture the Spalding.

The Great Pine Cone War.

The 1st Annual Sheep Creek Stick-Boat Race.

Wilderness Hide-and-Seek.

Cowboys and Indians.

The Great Pine Cone War, Part II.

Expedition Lagoon Stone-skipping Championship.

And finally The Great Slime-City Snake Hunt.

The sun was setting on the top of the Ponderosa pines to the west when the Lewis and Clark Squad settled down behind a crop of granite boulders at the base of Arrowhead Butte, only twenty yards from the fishing trail.

Jeremiah lay back in the pine needles. "I'm worn out. I haven't done so much running since I put the hot sauce on Mrs. Pointer's Burrito Surprise, and she made me run 100 laps around the gym."

Larry sat on his basketball. "I think it turned out to be a good workout."

"I don't think I've laughed this much in my life," Feather added. "This has been really cool, even if we didn't catch the international terrorists. Cody, this was a great idea."

"Hey, we still might see something," Jeremiah offered.

"We've got to meet Denver at the trailhead in less than an hour," Cody reported.

"Whatever they're going to do, it will be after dark." Larry leaned closer to the other three. "Raptors are always released at night!"

"Nothing to be afraid of," Jeremiah bantered. "We'll

just feed them Cody's cowboy sandwiches! That will stop them in their tracks."

"But we could get arrested for cruelty to animals," Larry cautioned.

"Well, it's the only thing we have left to eat," Cody added.

Jeremiah dove flat on his stomach behind the rocks. "Hit the deck. Someone's coming!" he whispered.

"I don't hear any—" Larry's sentence ended when Cody grabbed his shirt collar and toppled him into the pine needles next to the others.

"Didn't I tell you that it would be a piece of cake?" a male voice announced.

"Well, I did expect more security measures. That one put up quite a ruckus. Of course, I expected a greater number also," a woman responded. "Are you sure this was worth all the effort?"

Cody poked the others and mouthed the words, "It's them!"

"It's a symbolic gesture."

"Are you sure it's a big enough story for the newspapers to cover?"

Cody motioned for the others to stay down.

The man's voice was just above a whisper. "They will after I make the phone call. But I agree with you, it wasn't exactly what my informant reported it to be."

"Maybe you need a new informant," the woman replied. "How about releasing them right here?"

"This will be good. They can hide in the rocks until nighttime. Then they'll want to move down to the lake, I suppose."

Cody inched closer to the east side of the rocks. *What exactly is it that will hide in the rocks? I hope it's not snakes! Or tarantulas! Or Gila monsters. Or . . .*

"All right, gang, time to scatter! You're free! Go on . . . enjoy yourselves. In the name of LART you are free!"

His head inches above the pine needles, Cody peeked around the rocks. He watched the back side of two jeans-and T-shirt-clad figures hike back down the tree-lined trail toward the bridge. He held up his hand for the others to stay still.

When the two disappeared around the bend, Cody sat up.

Larry scampered down away from the rocks. Jeremiah and Feather brushed pine needles off their T-shirts.

"What are they, Cody?" Jeremiah quizzed. "Could you see what they turned loose?"

"No, let's take a look." Cody started to hike around the rock pile.

"Let's don't," Jeremiah objected. "I mean, you two go on. I'll check on Larry. I think he's sick."

Cody warned, "Whatever it is, don't scream. We don't want those two to hear us and come back up the trail."

Jeremiah scooted down the slope toward the lake. Feather slipped her hand into Cody's, her fingers gripping his tightly.

He gripped back as they stole around the corner of the ten-foot-high rock pile.

"What is it?" Jeremiah called out in a low voice.

When a head peeked out from the rocks, Feather gasped and gripped Cody's hand so hard he thought his fingers would fall off.

It had rich brown fur, short rounded ears, and dark eyes. The creature climbed on the large boulder on its short legs. Its long neck was decorated with a turquoise ribbon.

"Cody, what is it?" Feather whispered, now clutching Cody with both hands.

"It's Marvin!" he laughed.

"Who?"

"What is it, Cody?" Jeremiah called. "What do you see?"

Cody caught the animal by the nape of the neck and lifted it straight up into the air for Jeremiah and Larry to see.

"Marvin?" Jeremiah called out. "Are the others there?"

"I guess so."

Jeremiah trotted up the hill with Larry a few steps behind.

"Who's Marvin?" Feather asked. "What is it—a weasel?"

"This is Marvin the mink. Marvin, meet Feather."

"You know him?"

Jeremiah reached them. "Hey, Marv! How's it going, little buddy? Where are your brothers?"

The mink didn't reply but hung limply in Cody's grip.

"You mean, those guys were animal rights activists

who broke into a mink farm and rescued these little minks from being someone's fur coat?" Feather probed.

"They might be animal rights people, but this isn't exactly a mink farm. Poor Mrs. Carter. It will break her heart," Jeremiah responded.

"How do you know this one is Marvin?" Feather quizzed.

"Marvin wears turquoise; Melvin has green; Merlin wears yellow—," Cody revealed.

"No," Jeremiah corrected, "Myron has yellow; Merlin has orange."

"That's right." Cody nodded. "And Maurice doesn't wear a ribbon at all."

"How come?" Feather asked.

"Maurice has an attitude," Jeremiah informed her. "The other four are cream puffs."

"Time-out. Time-out," Larry called. "What's all of this about?"

"Feather's right. They thought they were saving animals from a cruel fate or something, so they set Mrs. Carter's minks free. I didn't even think about them the other day."

Another beady-eyed furball crawled out on a rock next to them. There was a yellow ribbon on its neck. Jeremiah reached down and grabbed it by the nape of the neck and held it in front of him. "All right, Myron, where are the others?"

"Larry, empty out the backpack. We'll keep them in there until we get them home," Cody directed.

"How come you know them all by name?" Larry asked.

"Me and Townie feed them for Mrs. Carter every Thanksgiving and Christmas when she goes to Seattle for the holidays."

"So they're just pets?" Feather queried.

"Yeah. Mr. Carter bought six kits about ten years ago. He was going to start a mink farm. But then he found out the guy who sold them to him had sold him six males."

Feather reached out and petted Marvin on the top of the head. "That ended the mink farm idea?"

"Yeah, and one of them died that first year." Carrying a mink in one hand, Cody searched the rocks for more. "So Mr. and Mrs. Carter just raised the five males for pets. She puts ribbons on them so folks can tell them apart."

"But Maurice doesn't like wearing a ribbon?" Feather asked.

"Maurice doesn't like being a mink. He thinks he's a watch dog. He chases cars and everything," Cody explained.

When a green-ribboned mink crawled out beside Cody, he reached down and snatched it up with his left hand. "This is Melvin. He's the littlest, so he's spoiled."

"He's spoiled? And the others aren't?" Feather asked.

"Melvin gets to stay in the house."

"The lady keeps a mink in her house?"

"Just Melvin," Cody replied. "See, about five years ago Mr. Carter died, so Mrs. Carter is all alone out there except for her minks."

"They aren't exactly wild minks," Feather observed.

"Hardly. And they aren't being abused. I have a feeling if minks could vote, they'd all want to be adopted by

Mrs. Carter. These guys don't know anything but living with her."

Jeremiah reached down and snatched up a furry varmit wearing an orange ribbon. "Here's Merlin. He's the tubby one. Mrs. Carter has been trying to talk him into going on a diet."

"Are you going to take them back to her?" Feather asked.

"I think it's best for them and for her, don't you? It's not illegal for her to own a mink, any more than it is to own a horse or a dog."

"Yeah. They probably won't know what to do out here," Feather agreed.

"Okay," Larry asked, "they set the minks free. But what does that have to do with an election?"

"Must be a LART election someplace." Feather shrugged.

"Lart? What is that?" Cody inquired.

"Let Animals Roam Today!" Feather informed him. "Haven't you ever heard of LART?"

"I don't guess so," Cody admitted.

"Floppy was a charter member of LART."

"The girl with the squished bunnies?"

"That was an unfortunate accident," Feather corrected.

"It was unfortunate, but no accident. They were released on purpose. So were Mrs. Carter's minks," Cody asserted.

"Someone abandoned these little guys just to win an election?" Larry pressed.

"Yeah, I guess. But they probably didn't know they were pets," Cody countered.

Feather pointed to Marvin. "The ribbons around their necks should have been a clue."

"Whatever," Cody responded. "Let's put them in the backpack and see if we can find Maurice."

Cody swung the green canvas backpack to his back, and Jeremiah deposited the four mink into it. Soon four little brown heads bobbed up behind Cody's.

"They're cute!" Feather giggled.

"Aren't you afraid you'll get rabies?" Larry cautioned.

"Not from these guys," Cody contended. "They have their shots every year during their annual checkup by the vet."

"These are the most tame wild animals I've ever seen." Feather reached over and scratched Merlin's head. He sniffed and searched her hand for something to eat.

Cody continued to explore the rocks. "Except for Maurice."

"We won't catch him without bait," Jeremiah cautioned.

"What have we got left to eat?"

"Nothing but Cody's sandwiches," Larry disclosed.

"The humane society would arrest us," Jeremiah hooted.

"We don't have any choice. You know Maurice won't come out unless there's food," Cody said.

"Or a car to chase," Jeremiah chuckled.

"Over here!" Feather called out. "I see some eyes peeking out over here! Is that him?"

Cody stared down into a dark crevice between three giant boulders. "Yeah, that's some kind of varmit. Townie, toss a piece of that sandwich back in there and then put some more out on this rock. Maybe that will lead him out."

"This is the meanest thing I ever did to an animal!"

"Those sandwiches aren't that bad!" Feather protested.

"Here he comes!" Jeremiah called out.

"You want to get him, Townie?" Cody asked.

"No way. Maurice never did like me."

"He doesn't like anyone except Mrs. Carter. Here, you carry the boys. I'll try to nab Maurice," Cody offered.

When the ribbonless mink crept out on the rock, it stared right at Cody.

"Hey, he remembers you!" Larry acknowledged.

"That's what I'm afraid of!"

Just as the animal latched onto the sandwich, Cody snatched him up by the back of the neck. The three-and-a-half-pound furry animal with white spots on his stomach tried to spin around and claw at Cody.

"You're not going to put him in here, are you?" Jeremiah panicked.

"Nope. I'll just carry him. Larry, give him more sandwich."

"Give him? Me?" Larry tossed the rye bread sandwich toward the dangling mink. The top slice of bread tumbled to the dirt, but the bottom half with the unsalted peanut butter reached the mink, who clutched it to his face.

"Hey, he quit kicking!" Cody exclaimed.

Most citizens around Halt, Idaho, missed viewing one of the summer's more hilarious sights. In the twilight of an August evening, it was already too dark to see Denver Clark's Dodge pickup tooling out to Mrs. Carter's place east of town. Next to Denver sat Feather Trailer-Hobbs, and riding shotgun was Larry Lewis.

But the real excitement was Jeremiah Yellowboy perched on a spare tire in the back of the pickup with four slightly curious, slightly nervous mink peering out of the top of his backpack. Next to him sat Cody Wayne Clark, his hand extended away from his body. Maurice the mink dangled in the evening breeze. He clutched to his breast and face half a peanut butter and jalapeño sandwich—on rye.

Mrs. L. J. Carter and her 1972 Lincoln were not at home when they arrived. Cody and Jeremiah deposited the backpack tenants in the mink house that sat on the old farmhouse's gigantic front porch.

Maurice sprinted under the porch, dragging his treasure.

"Do you think she's out looking for the boys?"

"The boys?" Feather asked.

"She calls the minks her 'boys,'" Jeremiah reported.

"Why don't you leave her a note?" Denver suggested. "I need to get home."

Cody heard a roar on the dirt road leading to the Carter farm as headlights approached. "Here she comes!"

"How can you tell that's her?" Larry quizzed.

"Because it's a wide old boat of a car, and it's being driven too fast."

"That's Mrs. Carter all right!" Jeremiah laughed. "Don't ever let her give you a ride to town. It's scary."

The big, dark-colored Lincoln skidded to a stop in front of the house. A white-haired woman wearing a Seattle Mariners baseball cap emerged with a wide smile on her face.

"Well, I didn't know I had company. I wouldn't have stayed at the bowling alley so long! What's the occasion, cowboy?"

"Have you been gone all day?" Cody asked.

"Yes, I went to Lewiston to shop and practice bowling. A 161 average today. Not bad for a gal who's seventy-eight."

"That's amazing!" Larry muttered.

She stepped closer. "I don't know everyone."

"These are our friends Larry and Feather."

"I'm glad to meet you. Did you bring them out to see the boys?"

"Yes," Feather replied, "I'd never seen minks before."

Mrs. Carter walked over to the steps of the wooden porch, and Melvin, Marvin, Myron, and Merlin lined up expectantly.

"I suppose Maurice is under the porch?"

"Yes, ma'am. He drug something under there."

"Maurice," she called out, "don't play with your food. Whatever you have, you eat it! No more dead animals under the porch!"

A noise halfway between a squeal and a hiss filtered up through the worn boards of the porch, which was followed by a buzz from the Lincoln.

"Whoops, that's my cell phone. Just a minute, kids."

While Mrs. Carter retreated to her car, Feather huddled near Cody. "This isn't your typical old lady, is she?"

Cody grinned. "She's one of a kind."

Mrs. Carter marched back over to the Squad, carrying her cellular phone. "I don't know why I have one of these. I don't get many calls, and when I do, they can be pretty wild."

"Who was on the phone?" Feather asked.

"A reporter for the *Examiner*. He said they received a cryptic message a few minutes ago that some group named Kart or Dart or . . . Lart . . . that's it. Some group called Lart claims to have raided a mink farm in the area and set the prisoners free. They called me to see if I knew anything about it."

"What did you tell them?" Feather asked.

"I told them there wasn't a mink farm for 100 miles, and all my boys were sitting right here on the porch. They figured it was just a crank call. Maybe some college kids with a false alarm fraternity stunt during rush week." She stared down at the four mink on the porch. "I wait on those five boys day and night. Now just who is the prisoner here?"

"We've got to get home now, Mrs. Carter. Denver's waiting for us in the truck," Cody announced.

"I'm sorry Maurice is so inhospitable," she apologized. "I'll talk to him about that later. But this way he won't try biting your tires when you leave."

Seven

The way I have it figured, we only have to win one more game, and we're in the championship!" Larry tossed his backpack out of the Clarks' Suburban and waited for the others to grab their gear.

Jeremiah's backpack had colorful powwow patches sewn all over it. "How do you figure that?"

"Because we've beaten these teams before. If we win one, the worst we could do is have four losses. The only teams left that could possibly end the season with four losses are teams that we've beaten twice. Therefore, if we tie, we would get to play in the championship. We're goin' to do it, gang!" Larry encouraged them.

Feather's backpack was homemade of beige ducking and had the words "Save a tree, save the planet" embroidered on it. "Yes, well, we'll have to play the Ponderosa Pirates in the championship game. Rocky, J. J., and Devin have beaten us twice this summer."

"Ah, but they didn't know about our secret weapon," Larry triumphed.

Cody grabbed his drab, worn olive green backpack and slung it over his right shoulder. "What's our secret weapon?"

"We now have undisputedly the toughest kid in Halt on our team!"

Cody stared up at the railroad trestle halfway up the mountain in front of them. *Yeah, well, the toughest kid in Halt is at the moment scared spitless. I'm probably the only guy in town that would rather play the Pirates than hike over Deception Pass.*

After a brief safety lecture from Cody's mother, the four were left at the base of Tamarack Ridge.

Larry stepped up beside Cody. "What's the plan, Capt. Clark?"

"This is Townie's deal, not mine."

Jeremiah stared at the steep hillside in front of them. "Well, my plan is that we hike straight up to the trestle and then just follow the tracks over Deception Pass—that's all. What do you think, Cody?"

"Let's take one step at a time. The first thing is making it up to the tracks. I think we'll need to zigzag back and forth up the grade. It's too steep to go straight up."

"Lead the way, cowboy!" Feather called out.

Cody stared at her.

"What's the matter? Is something wrong?"

"I guess I've never seen you in regular jeans before. You always wear shorts."

"Yeah, well, I was *told* that we all needed to wear jeans because of the brush on the mountain. It's probably a great disappointment that you don't get to ogle my fabulous legs!"

"What? I didn't mean . . ." Cody gulped. "Come on, let's go."

"I think he looks good with a red face," Feather smirked. "Don't you, Townie?"

"Everyone looks better with a red face," Jeremiah laughed.

"Well, this is a day for firsts," Feather continued. "It's my first day all summer to wear long pants, and it's the first time Larry has gone anywhere without his basketball."

"What do you think is in my backpack?"

"Noooo! Why?" Feather asked.

"Because you never know when you'll run across a court and an empty hoop."

"On Deception Pass?" Jeremiah quizzed.

"Who knows?"

They climbed over several boulders and reached the steep ascent of Tamarack Ridge. "Save your strength. Don't talk much. It will be the steepest climb of the day just to reach the tracks," Cody advised.

The bare mountainside had no trees, but foot-tall brown grasses grew sparingly out of thin topsoil and crumbling granite. Outcroppings of rock littered the landscape. Cody fell into a pattern of climbing on an angle to the right fifteen steps, then back fifteen steps to the left. After each three repetitions of this process, he declared a two-minute rest.

By the second rest, sweat rolled down his face. He pulled off his straw cowboy hat and wiped his forehead on his shirttail. By the fourth rest, his black sleeveless T-shirt was wringing wet. Jeremiah dug into his pack for his water bottle.

"Take it easy on the water," Cody cautioned.

"I thought you said there was fresh water at Brown Bear Springs," Feather commented.

"There is, but if we drink too much, we'll get cramps before we ever reach the tracks."

"Yeah," Jeremiah agreed, "and the only thing worse than climbing up Tamarack Ridge is climbing down it."

Cody looked back down the Ridge to the dirt parking area where they had begun. *No, there are things worse than going back. Hiking through tunnels, for instance.*

It was after 11:00 A.M. when Cody pushed the others up to the railroad tracks. He had hiked back down the final thirty feet of the ascent and, placing his hand in the small of their backs, he dug in his boots and shoved them, one at a time, up the steep mountain.

All four collapsed in the middle of the tracks.

"I have never been so tired in my entire life!" Jeremiah gasped.

Larry nodded his head. "My legs are killing me!"

Feather pointed to the base of the grade. "Look down there! We really climbed a steep mountain, didn't we?"

"I've got an idea—let's forget Deception Pass and hike downhill to Culdesac. We can call my dad from there," Larry suggested.

"No way," Jeremiah protested. "We're going over Deception Pass. This is a once-in-a-lifetime event. It's something we can tell our grandkids about."

Cody yanked his hat off and squirted bottled water on top of his head. *If we live long enough to have grandkids. Lord, this is getting serious. Don't You think now would be a good time to deliver me from this fear?*

"Anyone want some unsalted almonds?" Feather asked. "They can give you quick strength."

"It will take a lot of strength to get me going!" Larry moaned. "Maybe we should stay here and let a helicopter rescue us."

Jeremiah reached into his pack and pulled out a candy bar and then smiled at an imaginary camera. "Not going anywhere for a while?"

Their two-minute rest turned into a ten-minute rest, but when they finally began their hike along the abandoned Central Prairie Railroad tracks, they found the climb manageable.

Jeremiah now led the way. His brown arms glistened with sweat. His Chicago Bulls red tank top clung to his body. His old, faded black and gold Halt High School Hawks baseball cap was turned, bill back. His white-toothed smile reached from ear to ear.

Larry tramped behind him. Dangling from his neck was a clear plastic compass, and crammed on his head, a crisp red and white U.I. cap. He held his hands straight out to balance himself as he strolled on top of the left iron rail. "A hundred!" he shouted. "I've made it over a hundred railroad ties without stepping off! Cool, huh? I wonder what the world record is? Am I good, or what? Maybe I ought to be in gymnastics. You know, I could do that balance beam thing. What do you guys think?"

"The balance beam is three or four feet off the ground. You're only six inches off the ground," Cody counseled.

"Maybe Larry's right," Feather concluded. "Go ahead, Larry; jump up in the air, flip a somersault, and come back down with your feet on the rail! Let's see how you do."

Larry stepped off the rail and tramped behind Jeremiah. "I changed my mind. Gymnastics would be too great a diversion from basketball. Maybe I should practice dribbling on the railroad ties. I wonder how long I could keep it going? I wonder what the world record is for rail-road-tie dribbling?"

Feather's pastel yellow T-shirt hung outside the narrow waist of her jeans. Cody watched her light brown hair bounce as she hiked ahead of him. It was pulled together at her shoulders by a fat blue rubber band. Her small beige straw hat had a narrow brim that was curled up with a bright artificial sunflower attached on the right side to the yellow ribbon hatband.

Cody tramped along behind the gang, his thumbs laced in his front jeans pockets. His fingers dangled, as did his thoughts. *Instead of going though the tunnel, I'll climb the peak. I can tell them it's something I've always wanted to do.*

Actually, Lord, I've never wanted to do it.

What's that verse? "Peace I leave with you, my peace I give to you." That's what I need, Lord. A nice peaceful day. No anxiety, no worry, no panic, no sweaty palms, no barfing, no fainting, no wetting my pants . . .

Besides, what can happen?

Okay, so the tunnel can collapse on me. There are worse

things than dying, right? Like being buried alive for three days and then dying! If you don't mind, Lord, there must be a better way for me to die.

Feather glanced back over her right shoulder. "Cody, what's heaven like?"

"Heaven?" he gasped. "Why are you thinking of heaven?"

"We are so high up compared to the road down there. It's like this is a trail to heaven. What's heaven like?"

"It has streets of gold," Jeremiah shouted back. "I know that much!"

"I wonder what the basketball courts are made of?" Larry asked as he hopped back up on the rail.

"What makes you think it has basketball courts?" Jeremiah queried.

"It wouldn't be heaven without a basketball court," Larry insisted.

"What do you think, Cody?" Feather pressed.

"Oh, I guess it's homey."

"Homey?"

"Yeah, it's Jesus' home, and He's getting it ready so we'll feel at home when we get there."

"That's a nice way of putting it."

"That's the way Jesus describes it in John 14. He ought to know. He's been there."

"Do you think about heaven much?" she asked.

"Sometimes. Why?"

"Well, suppose a person divorced his wife and married someone else."

"Someone much younger than him?"

She looked back over her shoulder. "Okay, suppose my dad marries this Brittany. When he gets to heaven, does he live with her or with me and Mom?"

Cody licked his chapped lips and stared across the canyon beneath them. "Eh, well, not everyone goes to heaven, of course."

"I know that much," she huffed. "But let's suppose all of us involved come to the place of accepting the Lord and end up in heaven."

"Heaven is different from here on earth," Cody disclosed.

"What do you mean, different?"

"Well, there is no marriage, no individual families. We're all one big family up there."

She stopped and stared back at him. "No marriages?"

"That's what Jesus said," Cody informed her.

Feather hiked along in silence as they approached the first trestle. All four stopped at the edge and stared through the wooden slats at Slab Creek far below them.

"Well," she blurted out, "if you and I aren't married in heaven, you'll at least show me around, won't you?"

"Married?" Jeremiah hooted. "You and Cowboy are going to get married? You're only thirteen."

"It might be ten years away, but a girl has to make plans. It's a cinch that boys don't make the plans."

"What do you think about that, Cody?" Larry asked.

"Let's hike single file along the walk ramp. It's probably best not to look down. Townie, do you want me to go first?"

Jeremiah turned to Feather. "I don't think he heard a word you said."

"That just goes to prove my point!" she stormed.

"What are you guys talking about?" Cody asked as he started across the eighteen-inch-wide walkway by the side of the trestle.

"About the future of Cody Wayne Clark. Nothing important," Jeremiah answered as he followed along the trestle.

"What do we do if a train comes along?" Larry piped up.

"Fall flat on your stomach and hold onto the walkway," Cody advised. "Of course, the track is abandoned, so there's no danger of that."

"Hey! Look at this!" Jeremiah called out as he leaned away from the wooden guardrail. He let a glob of saliva drool from his lips.

"That's totally gross!" Feather called out.

"Wow, I could see my spit go all the way to the creek! Cool, huh?"

"Hey, let's have a contest!" Larry ventured. "What do you say, Cody? Who can hit that big boulder in the middle of the creek?"

"You guys are extremely disgusting!" Feather gagged.

Larry and Jeremiah replied in unison, "Thank you. Thank you very much."

The tallest trestle, the one spanning Whitetail Creek, stands 106 feet high. The Lewis and Clark Squad crossed it holding hands and reciting aloud the Lord's Prayer. They ate lunch at Brown Bear Springs and then followed the tracks as they inched up the granite slope of Scout Cliff.

"It's not so bad if you don't look down." Feather's voice sounded shaky.

"But then you miss the view!" Cody exclaimed.

"Believe me," Larry called out, "I'm not missing anything!"

"Cody, wait a minute!" Feather cried.

"Keep going, Clark!" Larry hollered. "This thing has to end somewhere!"

"Cody," Feather begged, "hold my hand. Then I can look out away from the cliff without being afraid of falling."

"You aren't going to fall for that old trick, are you?" Jeremiah joshed.

"Speaking of falling," Feather continued, "I wonder what would happen if I gave the pride of the Nez Perce Nation a shove!"

"Keep hiking!" Larry pleaded.

"Please, Cody!" she called out again.

For the rest of the trip up the cliff, Cody and Feather climbed side by side, hand in hand. That is, until they reached the base of Deception Pass. Several scrub pines had sprouted around the mouth of the tunnel, and the climbers sat and rested in their shade.

Cody's hands began to shake.

Lord, I don't know what to do. This isn't funny. This is exactly what I've been dreaming about for a week. I can't go through there. I just can't. I know You've promised to be with me always. I know You'll look after me, but I just can't do it. I can't make myself. There's no way on earth.

"Cody, how come they call this Deception Pass?" Feather questioned. Then she added, "You really worked up a sweat on that grade, didn't you?"

Cody wiped his forehead on his shirttail and then picked up two golfball-sized stones and gripped them tightly. "Eh, well . . . from down there in the canyon, this looks like a pass over the mountains. I guess the old-timers tried to cross here to get up to the gold fields . . ."

"But," Jeremiah continued the story, "when they got about this high, they realized that the cliff went straight up from here. There's no way over at this point."

"So they called it Deception Pass?" Larry ventured.

"Yeah, but when they built the railroad about a hundred years ago, they blasted right through the granite and made a tunnel."

"It's not a very long tunnel, is it?" Feather queried.

Jeremiah pulled off his cap and ran his fingers through his butch haircut. "A half a mile or something. Right, Cody?"

"Yeah, I think so."

"Anyway, when the train was running, it was dangerous to hike through there. It's too difficult to maintain as a tunnel, so after they pull up the rails and ties, they're going to fill it up."

"So," Larry blurted out, "only a few people in history have actually hiked through Deception Pass!"

"Yeah, and after next fall, no one else ever will again," Jeremiah said.

"This is so cool." Larry added, "Man, I'm glad we got past that scary part. Come on, Squad, let's tackle the tunnel!"

"You know what we ought to do?" Feather suggested. "We should tie ourselves together with Cody's rope so we won't get separated once we're inside."

"No!" Cody shouted.

"But I thought—," Feather began.

"Everyone should go at his own pace," Cody insisted. "Then we'll meet on the other side."

"Whatever." Jeremiah shrugged. "We better dig out our flashlights." He stood and fished around in his backpack. Then he pointed the big black flashlight toward the yawning mouth of the tunnel. "I'll go first. Cowboy, you bring up the rear in case anyone needs your help."

"Yeah," Cody readily agreed.

"You two go on." Feather motioned to Jeremiah and Larry. "I'll hike with Cody."

"*No!*" Cody barked.

"What?" she questioned.

"Go with Larry and Jeremiah!"

"But I just—"

"You heard me—go on with them!"

Her eyes narrowed, and she folded her arms across her chest. "You don't talk to me in that tone of voice, Cody Wayne Clark!"

"I'm sorry," he muttered.

She stepped closer, and he tried to keep his hands and knees from shaking.

"Cody, are you all right?" she whispered.

He bit his lip and shook his head.

"Are you scared? It's those dreams, isn't it?"

He nodded.

"Let me help you!"

"I've . . . I've got to do this on my own," he choked.

"Is that because you're stubborn or too proud to admit you're afraid?"

"Please, Feather . . ." His voice was somewhere between a plea and a sob.

She studied his eyes. "Okay, cowboy, you're on your own. And don't worry, I won't tell Townie and Larry."

"Thanks, Feather-girl."

"If you aren't out ten minutes after I am, I'm coming back in to get you! You understand?"

"Yes, ma'am."

Then they were gone.

With a giggle, a shout, and the tramping of tennies, they all disappeared into the pitch-black mouth of the tunnel.

He turned around and looked back down the grade along the cliff. "This is stupid! I'll just go back down. But I can't go back. They'll be waiting for me at the other end. Why in the world did I ever agree to this?"

It's like I keep expecting You to come along, Lord, and deliver me, or I was hoping to wake up from a dream.

Cody slapped himself in the face.

But it's no dream!

He took a tasteless, tepid swig of water from his canteen and adjusted his pack. Something on the railroad track below him caught his eye.

Something's coming up behind us? Is that a little whitetail?

Cody pulled the brim of his hat down to shade his eyes.

Oh, no! A cougar! I can't believe this. It's my worst nightmare coming true. Lord, what are You doing to me? Do You hear me? This is not fun!

Cody flipped on his yellow flashlight and crept into the tunnel. He could hear the whispers and giggles of voices ahead in the darkness. As soon as the light from the tunnel entrance faded, he followed the flashlight's dim glow between the two rails. Taking one step at a time, he paused at each railroad tie before taking another step.

Off to the right he heard water dripping into a puddle. To the left it sounded as if something moved. He flashed the light in that direction but could see nothing but the tunnel wall.

Maybe that cougar came in here already and is waiting to pounce!

He turned the light toward his eyes.

These batteries are dying. They can't be dying! I took them fresh out of the package this morning! This is weird. This is really, really weird. It's like I knew it was going to happen this way. Lord, were You giving me a preview?

Oh, man, if a train comes through, it will be just like my dream! If a train comes, Feather, Larry, and Townie will be run over, too! That wasn't part of the dream, Lord!

I've got to catch up with them!

He sprinted along the tracks. Then his foot caught on something. He slammed facedown into the ground. The flashlight crashed and went black. The contents of his backpack tumbled out in the darkness over his head.

He gasped for breath.

I can't breathe! There's a rope around my neck!

Cody screamed for help, but not a sound came out of his mouth.

Lord, I don't want to die. Please . . . not now! God, I'm scared . . . and alone . . . and weak . . . and I can't do it on my own. I give up. If You're going to have this mountain fall on my head, or if I'm going to get run over by a train or ripped to shreds by a cougar, go ahead. Just do it quickly.

Oh, man, I can't even breathe!

Cody rolled to his back and gasped for breath. He reached to his neck and felt his coiled nylon rope hanging like a necklace.

It's my rope!

He sat up in the darkness and felt around. There was no more sound of voices.

They already made it out of the tunnel!

Water dripped to the right of him. The air was damp and tasted stale, like in a flooded basement. His hands felt scratched and muddy.

Okay, where's the flashlight?

Cody picked up several items that felt like stuff from his backpack. Then he discovered the flashlight in two pieces and only one battery.

Crawling on his hands and knees, he searched the surrounding area but found nothing except rails, ties, rocks, and mud puddles.

I'm not going to lie around waiting for something bad to

happen! I might as well get killed on my way out. But how do I know which way is out? I could have gotten turned around when I fell!

Wait. The water was dripping on my right, and it's still dripping on the right. Okay, so far . . . so good.

Cody crawled along the track on his hands and knees, straddling the left rail.

Lord, this looks really wimpy. But no one on earth can see it except for You!

His knees got sore. He stood and walked, slowly sliding his foot along the rail.

"Jesus loves me this I know, for the Bible tells me so!"

He stepped on something squishy and immediately froze. Reaching down, he felt the surface where he was standing.

Mud! There was a mud and rock slide in here, and it hasn't been cleaned out. Why should it be? It's abandoned. Where are the others? Maybe there's a way around it, but I can't see, and the tracks are covered. Maybe the tunnel's completely blocked! What happened to them?

Cody began to run up the muddy slope, his boots sinking deep into the muck. He held his hands straight out in front of him so he wouldn't run into the wall of the tunnel.

High up in the mud slide, he slipped to his knees. They began to sink into the mire.

Then a light flashed on the tunnel ceiling from somewhere over the crest of the mud slide.

He opened his mouth to speak. Suddenly a muddy hand came out of the darkness and slammed over his mouth, tugging him to the left.

Goosebumps shot down his back.

He tried to pull away. There were lips at his ear. Whispering.

"Cody Wayne, it's me! Don't say anything! We aren't alone in here!"

"Feather?"

"Shhh!"

She tugged him down off the mud slide.

"Come here! Keep quiet!"

A flicker of light revealed a large boulder that had broken off and lined the north edge of the tunnel. He could see Larry and Jeremiah crouching behind the rock.

"Cowboy, are we glad to see you!" Jeremiah whispered.

"What are we going to do?" Larry asked.

"What's happening? Why are we whispering? Where's your flashlights?"

"There is a car on the other side of this mud slide," Feather breathed.

"A car? A railroad car?"

"No, it looks like an old Volvo."

"In a train tunnel?"

"An abandoned train tunnel," Jeremiah murmured.

"If you get close enough, you can hear them arguing with each other," Jeremiah informed him.

"About what?"

"We don't know. We were afraid to go on. We were waiting for you. What took you so long?" Feather asked.

"I dropped my flashlight and lost a battery, so I had to feel my way along in the dark."

"Man, I'm glad you're here!" Larry croaked. "What should we do?"

They're happy to have me here? Not nearly as happy as I am to be here!

"Let's crawl up until we can hear what they're saying. What's that light on the ceiling of the tunnel? Maybe we can tell who it is."

"It's their headlights. I think they hit this slide from the other side and got stuck trying to drive over it."

Cody led the group as they inched around the mud slide crawling on their stomachs. Finally he could see the Volvo in the shadows. The headlights now pointed upward to the top of the tunnel, but they couldn't see who was inside. Cody caught only a few words of conversation.

He heard a man bellow, "And I say we needed to stay off the highway."

The woman countered, "And I say you're a complete loser!"

Cody crawled back a few feet to the others. "It's them!" he whispered.

"Who?"

"The ones who set the minks free. The man and the woman."

"Are you sure?" Larry pressed.

"Yep."

"Why are they in here?" Jeremiah wondered.

"They think they're avoiding arrest. But no one's even looking for them!"

Feather leaned close to Cody. "What will we do?"

"Crawl past them. If we stay low, I don't think they'll see us."

"What if they do?" Larry chirped.

"Pretend that you're a mink."

Feather's voice sounded nervous. "That's not funny."

"Look, they are busy arguing over what to do next. So let's get out of here."

"Maybe we should go back," Larry whispered.

"There's a cougar back there."

"You're kidding me!" Jeremiah gasped.

"Nope. I don't know about you guys, but I want out of this tunnel. Come on!" Cody urged.

"I knew you'd get us out," Feather whispered.

It felt like she kissed him on the cheek.

The Volvo was several feet up on the mud slide. By keeping against the wall and crawling on their stomachs through the mud puddles and dripping water, all four members of the Lewis and Clark Squad made it past the rig unseen.

"Is that the tunnel exit?" Larry whispered as they stood up and huddled fifty feet behind the car. "Is that a speck of light?"

"That's it!" Jeremiah exclaimed. He turned on his flashlight and pointed it toward the distant exit.

"Who's back there?" a man's voice shouted from the Volvo.

"Run!"

"Wait!" Cody called out, grabbing Jeremiah's flashlight. He cupped his right hand around his mouth like a megaphone and pointed the light straight at the man standing next to the car.

"This is the mpthffd Squad from Halt! We have you surrounded. Put your hands on top of the car and don't make any sudden moves!"

"What?" the man screamed. "Who are you?"

Jeremiah cupped his hands and shouted into the darkness, "I've got him in my infrared scope, sir. Shall I waste him?"

Their voices bounced and echoed off the rock walls of the tunnel.

"Wait!" Cody called. "Give them a chance to surrender first!"

A woman jumped out of the other side of the car and started climbing the mud slide. "Over here!" she shouted. "We can cross the mud slide on foot!"

The man dove into the car and turned off the headlights. "Wait up!" he hollered.

Now Cody could only see what Jeremiah's flashlight revealed—the back of the Volvo.

"Shall I fire, sir?" Jeremiah shouted.

"Fire!" Cody hollered.

Almost in unison, all four scooped up rocks and threw them in the direction of the little car. The noise of the rocks bouncing off the car echoed throughout the tunnel.

"After them, men!" Cody shouted. "Shoot on sight!"

Then he turned around and began to jog toward the distant exit. The others matched him step for step.

It was without question the sweetest breath of air Cody had ever filled his lungs with in his life. The sun was brighter, the sky bluer, the pine trees greener.

Feather looked prettier than he had ever seen her. She was, however, covered with mud from hat to shoes.

As were he, Jeremiah, and Larry.

Cody didn't stop jogging until they reached the tree line a quarter of a mile below the tunnel exit. He gasped for breath and collapsed into the pine needles beneath a grove of six-foot seedlings.

"We did it!" Jeremiah triumphed. "We hiked over Deception Pass!"

"We made it past those two in the car," Larry shouted. "That was the most cool thing I ever did in my life! It was like a James Bond movie!"

"Those guys were a piece of cake," Cody asserted.

"Yes, once again Cody Wayne Clark is our fearless leader."

"There was nothing fearless about it. After that dream about the tunnel, I was so terrified I almost had a heart attack."

"Really?" Larry questioned.

"Yeah. But by the time I got to you guys, I just didn't have any scared left."

"Shall we keep going?" Feather asked.

"Yeah. If that cougar's still at the other side, they might be hightailing it back out this way."

"There's really a cougar out there?" Jeremiah gulped.

"Yep." Cody stared down at the other three. "You guys

are the dirtiest, muddiest, messiest Squad I've ever seen in my life!"

A harmonious trio replied, "Thank you. Thank you very much."

"We can stop by Warm Springs and try to clean up a little before we make it back to the highway," Cody suggested.

On the hike down, Cody scooted over next to Feather and murmured, "Why did you kiss me when we were back in the tunnel?"

"What?" she gasped.

"You know, when you kissed me on the cheek?"

"You've got to be kidding," she thundered.

Jeremiah turned around. "What's going on?"

"The cowboy is delirious. He thinks I kissed him when we were in the darkness of the tunnel. Dream on, Cody Wayne!"

Beneath the mud pack Cody's face began to heat.

You know, Lord, dying in a tunnel isn't the worst thing that could happen to a guy!

For a list of other books by
Stephen Bly
or information regarding speaking engagements
write:
Stephen Bly
Winchester, Idaho 83555